The night breeze blew coolly against his heated skin.

And for a long while, Boone and Tara just stood there, frozen in time. The make-or-break moment. Would he be strong enough to stop this and walk away before he did something he would regret?

He'd been resisting Tara's allure for weeks, heck, months even. Trying to convince himself that getting together with her would be a bad thing.

His body didn't care about reasons or excuses. It was too late for either, his brain issuing a primal message he was helpless to resist or deny.

His arms tightened around her.

She went up on tiptoes and leaned into him.

Turn back. Turn back. It's still not too late. Just let her go. Move away.

But darn his Montana hide, he did not let her go. He did not turn away. He did not walk off. Instead Boone did what he'd been struggling hard not to do....

He kissed her.

Dear Reader,

What could be more fun than a road trip?

That is the question that led me to the premise of my new series, Stop the Wedding! Since it's a three-book series, I thought why not have three different kinds of road trips? One by land, one by sea, one by air. All with the same objective: to stop a wedding. And the wedding they're trying to stop is the marriage of Jackie Birchard and Coast Guard Lieutenant Scott Everly from *Born Ready*.

So to answer the question in *Night Driving*, what could be more fun than a road trip? Why, take one drop-dead handsome, broody former Green Beret in desperate need of love in his life. Add in one good-hearted dizzy hairdresser on a move from Bozeman, Montana, to Miami, Florida. Mix well and you have chemistry that lights up the night sky.

I hope you enjoy *Night Driving*, and that you'll be on the lookout next month for *Smooth Sailing*, the second book in the Stop the Wedding! series. If you're on Pinterest, drop by my *Night Driving* board to see the collage I made of Boone and Tara's trip @ http://pinterest.com/loriwilde/night-driving/.

Until then, happy reading!

Lori Wilde

Night Driving

—

Lori Wilde

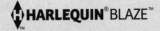

Recycling programs
for this product may
not exist in your area.

ISBN-13: 978-0-373-79741-7

NIGHT DRIVING

Copyright © 2013 by Laurie Vanzura

Printed in U.S.A.

ABOUT THE AUTHOR

Lori Wilde is a *New York Times* bestselling author and has written more than forty books. She's been nominated for a RITA® Award and four *RT Book Reviews* Reviewers' Choice Awards. Her books have been excerpted in *Cosmopolitan, Redbook* and *Quick & Simple.* Lori teaches writing online through Ed2go. She's also an RN trained in forensics and she volunteers at a women's shelter. Visit her website at www.loriwilde.com.

Books by Lori Wilde

HARLEQUIN BLAZE

 *The White Star
 **The Martini Dares
 †Perfect Anatomy
 ††Uniformly Hot!

To get the inside scoop on Harlequin Blaze and its talented writers, be sure to check out blazeauthors.com.

To all the servicemen and women
who give their lives to their country.

1

FEELING LIKE Jimmy Stewart in *Rear Window,* ex-Army Captain Boone Toliver stared glumly out at the treelined neighborhood as he sat on his front porch in Bozeman, Montana.

His right knee, fresh from a third surgery and wrapped in a stabilizing brace, lay propped up on a hassock. On the small table beside him sat a cell phone, a can of beer and a bottle of pain pills. He was trying to see if the beer would take the edge off his misery before surrendering to the medication. Although he knew well enough he wasn't supposed to mix the two, he was a big guy in a world of hurt. Not all of it physical.

Third time's a charm, the orthopedic surgeon had said.

It better damn well be. If not, he would never fully gain back the mobile life that a bomb in Afghanistan had stolen from him. For now, he had to hire someone to do everything—grocery shopping, housecleaning, chauffeuring him to doctor's appointments.

Not that money was an issue. Along with this house,

his father had left him over a million dollars. Boone had invested wisely; he was set for life, even if he never worked again. Although he'd much rather still have his dad around than any amount of money.

Plus, he was not an idle guy. He was at the end of his tether with this invalid malarkey. He had read books until his vision blurred, played video games until his thumbs ached and watched movies until his brain complained. All of his friends were military, and now that he was out of the service and injured to boot, their visits had become less and less frequent. He was no longer one of them.

Boone was bored, bummed out and bitter.

Not an attractive combo. He realized that, but he couldn't seem to snap himself out of the doldrums. This surgery was his last chance to reclaim what he'd lost. This time he was determined to follow doctor's orders to a T. Which meant sitting here twiddling his thumbs and watching the world pass him by.

Awfully hard for a man who'd spent a big chunk of his adult life at war.

He picked at the Velcro strap on his knee brace, pulling it off, then pressing it back down, then pulling it off again just to hear the crinkly, ripping noise it made as the two pieces separated. The sound underscored the monotony of his life.

A few houses over a couple of kids shot hoops in their driveway. The steady strumming of the basketball against cement made him nostalgic. Once upon a time, he'd been one helluva basketball player, but those days were long gone. The scent of supper hung in the air as the summer sun headed west. Idly, he thought about getting up and sticking a frozen dinner in the microwave, but he couldn't seem to drum up enough enthusiasm for even that task.

He took a swallow of beer and tried not to think about the throbbing in his knee.

An older model Honda Accord crawled down the block and then pulled into the driveway of the ranch-style bungalow across the street. His ditzy neighbor, Tara Duvall, got out of the Accord. Quickly, Boone picked up his cell phone and pretended to be deep in conversation, but his ruse didn't thwart Tara.

She raised her hand in greeting, gave him that radiant smile she was constantly flashing. Hell, he needed sunglasses and a bulletproof vest against her obnoxious cheerfulness.

"Hey, Boone." She wore a skimpy little halter top and cutoff blue jeans that hit her midthigh.

He tried not to notice just how tanned and supple those long, lean legs were. Or how, when she moved, that halter top with a handkerchief hem fluttered up enough to give him a glimpse of her gold navel ring. Her abdomen was taut and flat, her skin flawless. His mouth went dry and he felt an unwanted stirring below his belt. Annoying she might be, but the woman possessed a killer body.

Block the urges, Toliver. Sure, she's sexy, but she's not worth the aggravation.

She toddled across the street toward him in wedge sandals that were far too high for her petite build, but somehow she managed to walk in them with startling grace.

Frick. She was coming over.

Frowning, he held up the phone for her to see and waved her away, then stuck the phone back to his ear. "Yes, uh-huh." He feigned conversation.

Tara was one of those breezy, gabby women who could talk the hind leg off a mule. The last thing he wanted was to hear one of her upbeat, riotous stories about what had gone on at the hair salon where she worked. She was funny, impulsive, lively and reminded him far too much of his ex-wife. Spontaneous gals were nothing but trouble. Still, his body responded at her approach and he resented the heck out of her because of it.

She tiptoed up on the porch, an index finger laid over her lips.

"You don't say," Boone spoke into the phone.

She hitched her butt up on the porch railing, legs dangling off, blues eyes dancing with mischief.

Go away. He was not in the mood for Pollyanna.

"Yes, yes." He nodded as if someone on the other end of his fictitious conversation had just said something he could really support.

Tara's gaze skated over his injured knee. She pursed her lips in a pity pout, but then took in the beer and the bottle of pain pills. Her sympathy disappeared— thankfully—into a concerned scowl. She made a shame-on-you gesture, scraping one forefinger crossways over the other.

Buzz off, brat.

"Hang on a minute," Boone said to his imaginary caller. He put his palm over the phone, met Tara's eyes. "This conversation is going to go on for a while."

"I don't mind waiting."

What the hell did she want? "I mind."

"Private conversation?"

"Yeah."

Her lips were glossy cotton-candy-pink and her hair was four or five different shades of blond. Streaked in that chunky way that was popular these days. A modest dolphin tattoo graced her left shoulder and numerous earrings lay nestled in each ear. Her toenails were painted an alarming shade of aqua, and on the second toe of her right foot a gold toe ring spelled out LOVE.

"I'll go water your shrubs while you're talking," she said. "They look thirsty."

"No, no." He didn't want her doing him any favors. "Leave it be."

"Okay." She held up her palms. "Didn't mean to tread on your pride."

Glowering, he pressed the cell to his ear again. "I'm back," he said, feeling stupid for having gotten trapped into a fake phone call.

Well, if you could try just talking to her.

Except that never worked. Give her an inch and she took a mile. If he struck up a conversation, she'd plunk down on the porch beside him for hours as if they were friends or something.

That's when the phone rang for real.

Tara's lips formed a humorous O and her eye twinkled. "Oh, dude, you're so busted." She did the finger-shaming gesture again. "You were trying to avoid talking to me."

"Yes, and I really am on the phone now," he snapped and pressed the talk button without bothering to look at the caller ID. "Hello?"

"Boone?"

"Jackie? Hold on a second." He covered the receiver again. "It's my sister. Could we have this conversation later?"

"You have a sister?"

"Half sister."

"I didn't know that."

"There's a lot of things you don't know about me."
Thank goodness for that.

"You never talk about her."

"I never talk about her to *you*."

"Touché," she murmured, but she looked slightly wounded.

He forced a smile past his injured-war-veteran grouchiness. "Right now I just want to talk *to* her, if you don't mind."

"Sure." She shrugged. "I only came by to tell you that I'm moving away."

Yay! No more nosy neighbor butting into his business, throwing noisy late-night parties, no more bringing over casseroles and lecturing him on proper recycling techniques. But even as he thought it, Boone felt something else entirely. A strange, soft sadness. It was the same kind of melancholy that used to come over him every Sunday afternoon when he was a kid, knowing that the weekend was over, and he had to go back to school the next day.

Part of him almost told her to wait, but he managed to squelch the impulse. "See ya."

"See ya," she echoed and hopped from the railing.

He watched her lope across his lawn, her fanny swaying in those snug-fitting shorts. Mesmerized, his gaze locked helplessly on Tara's delectable butt.

"Boone? You still there?"

"Yeah, yeah, I'm here." He hitched in a deep breath and turned his full attention to Jackie. "Hey, sis. Long time no hear."

"I've been really busy," she said, sounding oddly giddy. Normally his sister was intense and serious. Her father was the famed oceanographer Jack Birchard.

Jackie had followed in his footsteps and she was working on her PhD.

Boone realized it had been over four months since he'd spoken to her and he hadn't told her about the third surgery. He hadn't wanted her to worry. They hadn't grown up together and they had really only gotten in touch with each other as teenagers when they'd bonded over the fact that their flighty mother had abandoned them both to their respective fathers. But Jackie was as resilient as Boone. They'd survived and thrived.

That is, he'd thrived until the damn bomb blast.

"What's up?" he asked.

"I'm getting married!" Jackie announced.

"Married?" he echoed, stunned. "To who?"

"You don't know him. His name is Scott Everly and he's a lieutenant in the Coast Guard."

"Jackie, seriously? A coastie?"

"What's wrong with a coastie?"

Boone wasn't going to get into the fact that he didn't consider Coast Guard *real* military. "I can't see you as a military wife. In fact, I can't see you as a wife at all."

"What does that mean?" All the joy escaped from his sister's voice.

Don't be a jerk, Toliver. Apologize. "Your career means so much to you."

"Yes, what's that got to do with anything? Are you saying that I can't have a meaningful career and be married at the same time?"

"How are you going to do research if you're following him around from post to post?"

"He's stationed in DC. Any promotions will just take him further up that chain. Besides, Scott is fully supportive of my career. He understands that there may be times when we'll have to be separated."

"How long have you known him?" Boone asked, feeling protective. She *was* his baby sister. He hated the thought of her making the same marital mistake he'd made. No matter how you sliced it, divorce hurt. He'd do whatever he could to save her from that heartache.

She didn't answer him.

"How long have you known him?" Boone repeated.

"You're being a jerk."

"You're not answering the question."

"A little over a month," she finally admitted.

"What!"

"Don't go ballistic. I know what I'm doing. Scott is the best thing that's ever happened to me. He's smart and kind and he loves the ocean as much as I do and—"

"Are you insane? Didn't you learn anything from my experience with Shaina—"

"I'm not you, Boone," she snapped. "And Scott isn't Shaina. This is real love, not some hot, horny, drunken Vegas hook-up on the eve of your enlistment—"

"Listen to yourself. Real love? You've only been dating the guy a month. He could be a serial killer for all you know." Boone clenched a fist, quelled the urge to jump up and start pacing.

"Six weeks. I've known him six weeks."

"Oh yeah, my mistake. Two weeks makes all the difference. Why didn't you say so?"

"I thought you'd be happy for me. I finally found someone who means as much to me as the ocean."

"You know exactly who you're acting like, don't you?"

"Don't say it," Jackie growled.

"Miranda."

"I am *nothing* like our mother."

He knew he'd struck a chord but for some unfathomable reason he just kept pushing. "Miranda married my dad after only knowing him for two months. How long did she date Jack before she plunged into that relationship? Six weeks, wasn't it?"

"I cannot believe you're reacting this way."

Boone couldn't believe it either. What was the matter with him? His knee hurt like a son-of-a-bitch, but that was no excuse. He could hear tears in her voice and that alarmed him. Jackie was a tough cookie. She didn't cry easily.

You, Toliver, are the world's biggest loser.

"I'm sorry." He backed down. "You took me by surprise. Just tell me you're going to have a nice, long engagement to make sure this guy is really the one."

"We're getting married in Key West on Saturday on the Fourth of July."

"This Saturday? Are you out of your mind?"

"If you can be happy for me, then you're welcome to attend the wedding. It's at four o'clock on the *Sea Anemone* at Wharf 16," she said, referring to Jack Birchard's research vessel. "If not, then stay in Montana and stew in your own self-pity."

"Jackie, I—"

She hung up on him.

Boone swore under his breath and immediately called her back. She didn't pick up, letting the call go to voice mail. He tried three more times. She still did not answer.

A raw ache gnawed at the pit of his stomach. Disgusted with himself, he slung the cell phone across the yard.

Smart. Real smart. Now you gotta go get it.

Guilt was a rock on his shoulders. He pushed up from the chair, winced against the bolt of pain that shot up his leg. He stared at the steps, swallowed hard. Going down them would take forever. He blew out his breath.

And suddenly there was Tara.

Relief washed over him and he instantly hated the feeling. He didn't need to be rescued.

She bent down to pick up his phone, then raised her head, concern in her eyes. "Did you have a fight with your sister?" She mounted the steps to hand him the phone.

"Thanks," he said gruffly.

"You're welcome." She paused.

He said nothing.

"I guess you don't want to talk about it?"

"I don't."

She nodded, sank her hands on her hips. "Okay. If you want to talk, though, I'm here. At least, for another week."

"So," he said, searching for something to say. "You're moving."

"Uh-huh. Going back home. My mom's sick."

"I hate to hear that."

"Breast cancer, but they caught it early. She's gotta have chemo and radiation, but she's going to be okay. It's just that, well, when something like this happens, you start thinking about what's really important in life and there's nothing more important than family, so I'm moving back."

Boone almost said, "I'll miss you." But he bit down on his tongue to keep from uttering the words. He didn't even know why he'd thought of it. She mainly drove him crazy with her good-natured prying. "Thanks for getting my phone for me. That was nice of you."

"You're welcome. I can tell you've been having a tough time of it." Her gaze drifted to his knee brace.

"You're not nearly as gruff as you want everyone to think."

Jackie would disagree.

"I know you're the one who shoveled Mrs. Levison's driveway last winter." She nodded at the house of the elderly widow next door. "And that you got up at dawn to do it so she wouldn't catch you and try to pay you."

"Who, me?" He shrugged. "With this leg?"

"Probably one of the reasons you had to have a third surgery. You can't stay still."

Boone winced. She was right. "You're too darn nosy for my own good."

Their gazes met.

She raised a hand. "I have to go start packing."

"Have a safe trip."

"I'll come say goodbye before I leave."

"Okay," he said, because he didn't know what else to say.

A small furrow creased her brow. "Are you all right?"

"Never better."

"You're such a liar."

An involuntary smile twitched his lip. "I know."

She tilted her head, studied him like he was a sad case. "Take care of yourself, Toliver."

"Same to you, Duvall." He wished she'd go. Boone didn't want her watching him limp inside.

He waited until she'd disappeared before he crushed the empty beer can, scooped the bottle of pills off the table and dragged himself into his living room. He dry-swallowed one of the pills and grimaced. He was too antsy to sit, in too much pain to stand and too worried about Jackie to do anything else. He tried calling her again, but she wasn't answering. He left a voice mail apologizing for what he'd said and asked her to please call him.

He pictured her in Florida, telling her fiancé what a tool her big brother was. Who was Boone to think he had a right to dictate how she should live her life? He had no right, and yet he could not in good conscience let her marry in haste. He'd done it. Lived through the fallout. Didn't want her to make the same mistake. He had to see her face-to-face. Had to talk to this coastie she seemed hell-bent on marrying.

Things hadn't been easy for Jackie. Their mother might have stayed with her longer, but that only seemed to have messed with Jackie's head more. Boone considered himself lucky that he didn't even remember Miranda.

Jackie, on the other hand, had been ten when Miranda took off, leaving her to be raised by her demanding father. She'd spent her life trying to measure up to Jack Birchard, and she'd told Boone on more than one occasion that the only time she felt truly relaxed were the summers they spent together in Montana at their Aunt Caroline's lake house. Both of them kept hoping that one day Miranda would show up at her sister's house, but she never did.

Boone's dad had married Miranda right out of high school. He told Boone that he couldn't call the marriage a mistake, because if he hadn't married her, he wouldn't have such a wonderful son. Wade Toliver knew how to make a kid feel loved. He'd been a hardworking building contractor who'd scrimped and saved and invested in buying and flipping houses, and then he was smart enough to get out of real estate before the housing bubble hit. With a father like Wade, Boone had barely missed having a mother. His dad had taken him everywhere with him, showing him the ins and outs of home maintenance, teaching him right from wrong.

Yeah. He'd be ashamed of you right now.

Okay. He'd screwed up, but whether his sister knew it or not, Jackie needed his clear-eyed perspective. He had to get to Key West before the wedding and talk some sense into her. He glanced at his watch. Six-thirty on Monday afternoon. That didn't even give him five days.

His knee felt like it was set in cement. He eased down on the couch. How was he going to get to Key West? During his last surgery, he'd had problems with blood clots, and this time the doctor had told him that under no circumstances was he to fly, and he'd even discouraged long car trips as well. If Boone had to travel by car, he was supposed to stop frequently, get out and move around. But it wasn't as if he could drive himself all the way to Key West. Hell, he couldn't even drive himself to the grocery store. Pathetic.

He whipped out his cell phone and did a Google search for the distance from Bozeman to Key West. Twenty-three hundred miles. Approximately a thirty-eight-hour drive, and that wasn't factoring in any stops.

Dammit. He shoved a hand through the hair that had grown shaggy since he'd left the military.

How was he going to get to Key West? Call a car service? That would cost a frigging fortune. Yes, he had the nest egg his father had left him, but most of that was tied up in investments, and since he hadn't grown up rich, he was still tight with a dollar.

Which is more important? Money or keeping Jackie from ruining her life?

Jackie. No doubt about it.

He called the only car service in Bozeman and they

flat-out told him they wouldn't drive him to Key West. Now what? Hire someone to drive him? But who?

Too bad he couldn't find someone to carpool with who was already going to Key W. He could pay for their gas.

Good idea. Great idea, in fact. But where could he find someone from his area headed in that direction ASAP?

Back to the internet.

He'd give it a shot. If he didn't get a reply by tomorrow morning, he'd try to find someone who could drive him. Pushing himself up off the couch, he lumbered into the spare bedroom that he'd turned into an office. Angling his leg with care, he dropped stiffly into the chair and then booted up his computer.

He placed the ad on a number of sites, figuring it was a long shot. He ate dinner, packed a bag and then spent the rest of the evening fretting about Jackie. He tried calling her numerous times only to discover she'd turned off her voice mail. She was really steamed.

Bullhead. You got yourself into this, you better get yourself out.

He checked for a response to his ads. Nothing. Finally, he went to bed.

Boone woke up at his usual time. Five in the morning. He'd been out of the military for almost nine months, but he couldn't seem to break the early-rising habit. Routine served him well today. He needed to get a move on if he was going to find a way to Key West by four o'clock on Saturday. Maybe this Scott Everly was the real deal, maybe he wasn't, but Boone was determined to see for himself firsthand. He hadn't been able to look after Jackie when they were kids, but he was definitely going to make up for it now.

He had a breakfast of eggs and oatmeal, worked out his upper body with weights, took a shower and then went to the computer with little expectation of a reply. Already he was thumbing through a list of his acquaintances who might be in a position to drive him to Key West. The list was pitifully short.

He opened his email and *pop!*

There it was. A reply to his ad. Yes. Eagerly, Boone read the message.

I am moving to Miami next week. I can take you that far if your trip can wait until Monday.

Disappointment stiffened his spine. He posted back.

That's too late. Is there any way you can leave today instead of next week?

He pushed back from the desk, not expecting a quick reply, but the person must have been at his or her computer, because he'd no more than gotten to his feet than his computer pinged, letting Boone know that he had a new message.

Sorry, no, I still have to pack and load my things into a U-Haul. The soonest I could leave would be Thursday afternoon.

Boone did the math. If they left on Thursday afternoon and drove straight through they could arrive in Key West early Saturday morning, but with his knee, there was no way he could ride in the car for thirty-eight hours nonstop. He would have to factor in at least another day. The latest he could leave was Wednesday afternoon. He sat back down and typed.

What if I paid to have someone come pack your things and load the U-Haul today? Could you leave tonight?

Feeling antsy, he hit Send and waited.

Sounds like you have an emergency situation, but Mercury is in retrograde. I try not to travel when Mercury is in retrograde. It messes with travel plans.

Seriously? Was this person for real?

What if I threw in five hundred dollars on top of everything else? Will that overcome your fear of Mercury?

It went against his sense of economy, but this might be the only opportunity he had.

It took a few minutes, but then the reply came.

All right. You have a deal.

Relief had him splaying both palms across the top of his head. Whew.

Done, he wrote. Where do you live?

There was another pause, this time so long that he started worrying. Had he scared off the prospect? Maybe it was a woman leery of driving with a man she didn't know. He couldn't blame her. It was smart to be prudent. In this case, honesty was the best policy.

I'm a war vet with a bum knee so I can't drive myself. My sister is about to make a big mistake, marrying a guy she barely knows, and I need to get to Key West before the wedding to talk some sense into her.

He held his breath. If honesty didn't work, he was back to square one, and he was running out of time.

He stroked a hand over his jaw, drummed his fingers on the desk.

Come on, come on, just say yes.

He thought of Shaina, of how young and dumb they'd been, blundering into marriage without any real knowledge of what it meant to commit to one person fully and completely. Then he thought of Jackie, knowing how easy it was to fool yourself into thinking you were in love when it was nothing more than lust. He could not let her make a mistake this big. He had to get to Key West no matter what he had to do.

His computer pinged and he returned his attention to the screen.

Boone?

He blinked at his name. Who was this?

Yes.

Small world. It's me. Tara.

2

BOONE STOOD OFF to one side of Tara's driveway clothed in an army-green T-shirt and camouflage cargo shorts, his muscular arms crossed over his chest, supervising the movers like a high school principal monitoring the hallways. His brow was knitted in a dark scowl, his right leg encased in a heavy metal brace.

"Hey, Toliver. You oughta get a patent," Tara teased as she breezed past him, her arms loaded with boxes.

"Patent?" he growled. "For what?"

"That broody frown. James Dean and Marlon Brando combined got nothing on you."

His glower deepened.

"Yup, watch out, you're heading for Darth Vadar territory."

"Darth Vadar wore a mask."

"Exactly."

His face relaxed. Just a bit. "Total mystery."

"What is?" Tara loaded the boxes into the back of the U-Haul, turned and wiped perspiration from her forehead with the back of a hand.

"You."

She smiled big, pleased.

Boone shook his shaggy head, two months past the point of needing a good haircut. But that was okay. Overgrown hair gave a stylist something to work with. She canted her head and imagined how he'd look in different cuts—slicked-back undercut, Brit-rock indie, men's quiff. Who was she kidding? He'd probably spoil her fun and insist on a military buzz.

"It's not a compliment," he said.

"What are you so prickly about?" She dusted her hands against her back pockets.

"I hate this." He hissed the last word through clenched teeth.

"What?" She studied him. He was in so much pain— both physical and mental—that it wrenched her heart. But she also knew he had no use for pity. How many times had he rebuffed her when she'd tried to help? Boone was one of those proud protector dudes who thought he was invincible. He hadn't handled life's curveball very well. Poor baby.

"Having to stand here and watch you carry boxes when I should be the one doing it."

"Oh, so you're responsible for the whole world? Good to know."

"Not the whole world, just my slice of it."

"Newsflash, Hercules. I'm not part of your world and I'm perfectly capable of carrying my own boxes."

"If I were healthy you would *not* be carrying your own boxes."

"If you were healthy, I wouldn't be driving you to Miami. Besides, I'm not some helpless damsel. I know how to take care of myself."

"You sure know how to wound a man, Duvall."

"I'm not in the military. You can call me Tara."

"Okay, then let the men I hired do the heavy lifting...*Tara.*"

The sarcastic way he muttered her name didn't get to her. She knew he was a big softy underneath all the gruffness. She'd seen Boone tenderly cradle their neighbor's new baby when Mrs. Winspree had brought her infant over to show him off. She'd seen him struggle not to shed a tear at his father's funeral. Had watched him drive his friends away because he was too proud to admit he needed help. Whether he wanted to admit it or not, she was the one person who kept him from disappearing into himself completely, even though he did his best to keep her at arm's length. What would happen to him once she was gone? Probably turn into a hermit and holler at kids for walking across his lawn.

Tara smiled sweetly and gently bumped Boone with a playful hip as she walked past him on her way to the house for another load of boxes. It was her way of telling him everything was going to be okay, but she wasn't prepared for the blast of pure heat that shot through her at the contact or the low, throaty masculine sound of alarm that he made in response.

Quickly she sprinted off, her heart bounding erratically. She was in such a rush that she ran headlong into one of the movers. Reflexively, the guy wrapped an arm around her waist.

"Slow down there, sweetcheeks." The man possessed a chest like a brick wall, a Tom Selleck mustache and a red bandana wrapped around his bald dome. "Is there a fire someone didn't tell me about?"

"We're on a tight time schedule," she said. "Have to get a move on."

"Let me just check my magic watch." He pretended to consult an imaginary wristwatch.

"What?"

"It's telling me that you don't have any panties on."

"Yes I do," she blurted, then belatedly realized it was some stupid pickup line. Duh, how could she be so gullible?

His grin widened and he made a big show of shaking his imaginary wristwatch and holding it up to his ear. "Damn, it must be ten minutes fast."

Ha-ha. She got it. He was suggesting that in ten minutes he'd have her panties off.

"Dude." Tara fake chuckled, rolled her eyes and pushed back against his embrace. She was about to tell him he needed a course in how and where to pick up women, but she never got a chance.

Boone was there, clamping a hand on the man's shoulder. "Let go of her," he said in a voice as ruthless as the sound of a .45 Magnum round being chambered.

Instantly, Bandana Head released her, stepped back and raised his palms in a gesture of surrender. "Chill, man. Just a little harmless flirting. I didn't mean anything by it."

"Get out!" Boone commanded and pointed toward the door, his expression deadly.

"I'm sorry, man. I didn't mean anything by it. I didn't know she was your woman. I swear."

"She's not my woman, but that still doesn't give you the right to manhandle her." Boone's eyes narrowed to dangerous slits. Boone was big, but the bald guy was bigger and Boone had a bum knee.

The guy puffed out his chest. "She ran into me."

"Look, look." Tara winnowed her way between the two men. To Boone she said, "I did run into him. It was my fault." Then to the bald guy she said, "Dude, cheesiest pickup line ever and borderline offensive."

"Borderline!" Boone snorted.

"Okay, it was offensive, but I'm sure..." She waved a hand. "What's your name?"

"Rodney."

"That Rodney meant nothing by it."

"Didn't mean a thing." Rodney raked a lascivious glance over her body and Tara regretted her snug-fitting T-shirt. She'd worn it for Boone's sake, knowing that it clung to her curves. She never thought twice about being too provocative for the moving men.

"Out." Boone pointed toward the door. He plucked his wallet from his back pocket, peeled off two one-hundred-dollar bills and a fifty and thrust them at the man.

"Hey, the deal was for five hundred dollars."

"That was before you insulted Miss Duvall. You've only done half the job, that's all I'm paying for."

Rodney looked like he was going to protest, but then he shrugged. "Suit yourself. You're gonna have fun loading up that van with your gimp leg." He turned, hollered to his partner who was in the back room packing up Tara's home office, "C'mon, Joe, we're outta here."

"Wow," Tara said to Boone as the front door slammed behind Rodney and Joe. "That's one of the best jobs of shooting yourself in the foot that I've seen in a long time."

"What? I was supposed to stand by and just let him grope you?"

"He didn't grope me."

"He was inappropriate."

"He was, but it's not your place to defend me, Boone. I'm perfectly capable of taking care of myself."

He snorted, folding those steely arms over his chest, blocking her out.

"What's that noise supposed to mean?"

"I'm not going there." He limped over to the kitchen counter where boxes were stacked, half-filled with the dishes Rodney had been packing up.

Tara wasn't going to let him get away with that. She scurried after him. "Where aren't you going?"

He turned to face her. His dark eyes flashed a warning. "You can take care of yourself, huh?"

She squared her shoulders, drew herself up to her full five foot four. "Absolutely."

"Your faucet leaks."

"So what?"

"At the end of the month you're chronically low on cash from helping out your free-loading friends and you're forced to subsist on ramen noodles and food sample giveaways at the grocery store."

Tara cringed. It was true. "Times are tough. I can't turn my back on people in need."

"Not even when you're one of those people? I know that worthless boyfriend of yours cleaned out your savings before he left town."

A sick feeling settled in her stomach. "How do you know that?"

A rueful expression softened his angular mouth. "Mrs. Levison likes to gossip."

"It's not really any of your business."

"And yet you're always trying to meddle in mine. Face it, Duvall, you're too generous for your own good."

She notched her chin up. "I consider generosity a positive trait to have."

"Not at the expense of your own welfare. Do you

know how hard it is to sit across the street watching you making the same mistakes over and over?"

"No. How hard is it?" she asked impishly, hoping to get him off her case by embarrassing him. Humor was her weapon of choice.

It worked. Boone's face flushed. "Time's wasting," he mumbled.

"And you just made things worse by running off the movers."

"Hell, if you hadn't been so flirty, I wouldn't have had to run them off."

Oh no, he didn't just say that! Outrage shoved a cold barb down her spine. Chuffing out her breath, she sank her hands on her hips. It took a lot to piss her off, but seriously? He was making this her fault? "Excuse me?"

"You know what your problem is, Duvall?" he asked.

"You mean, besides being too generous?" Her tone was as cold and brittle as a Montana winter.

"You have no boundaries."

His criticism stung, but it wasn't the first time she'd heard something similar. Well, fudge crackers. She was who she was and if he didn't like her, he could kiss her derriere.

Her mind flashed to an image of Boone's lips planted on her bare backside and she instantly grew hot all over. See? No boundaries. The man made a good point. Damn him.

"You dress too provocatively. No wonder the mover was eyeing you like chocolate candy. Your shorts are too darn short."

Her head shot up and she caught Boone checking out her legs.

Holy ham sandwich! He was jealous!

Hmm. Tara suppressed a grin, touched the tip of her

tongue to her upper lip. "Sorry. I'm not going to wear a snowsuit just to suit you and I don't appreciate you making me feel badly about myself."

To his credit, Boone looked chagrined, but then he went and ruined it by saying, "I'm not responsible for how you feel. I'm just calling it like I see it."

"Hey, you're not my big brother."

"Thank God."

"Why do you say that? I'm a good sister. A great sister, in fact. I can play shortstop and I don't scream when my brothers put bugs down the back of my shirt, and I have cute girlfriends for my brothers to date and I—"

"Because if you were my sister, I'd be arrested for the thoughts I've been having about you."

"Oh." She blinked. Grinned. "What kind of thoughts?"

"Illicit thoughts."

Imagine that. She sidled closer. "*Real*-ly?"

Boone stepped back, shook his head. "Duvall, you have no boundaries."

"I have five siblings," she explained, not knowing why she bothered other than the supreme satisfaction of knowing that he wanted her. For months, she'd been trying to charm him, but he'd been immune. Or so she'd thought, but apparently he put up a good front. Yet here he was admitting he liked her when she was moving thousands of miles away. What lousy timing.

"Five? That's quite a brood."

"Three brothers, two sisters. When you grow up in a crowd, it's a free-for-all. Try riding in the back of a minivan where you can't move an elbow without smacking someone in the eye and you wouldn't have any boundaries either."

For the briefest moment, he smiled. "Hey, I was in the military. I can relate to cramped quarters."

"So why do you have a problem with no boundaries?"

"Because it feels…" He trailed off.

"What?"

"Where are you in the birth order?" he asked, changing the subject.

She let it go, even though what he had not said whetted her curiosity. "Third youngest or fourth oldest, however you want to look at it."

"Stuck in the middle, huh? That explains some things."

Tara frowned. "Yeah, like what?"

"The outrageous clothes, the way you change your hair color every time the wind blows, the in-your-face cheerfulness. It's all a bid to stand out from the pack."

"Seriously? We're doing this? Because if we're pointing fingers, boy, do I have some stuff to unload on you."

"I wasn't pointing fingers. Merely making an observation."

"Guess what? I have eyes. I've observed a few things about you, too."

His eyes narrowed and darn if he didn't looked amused. "Yeah? Let's have it."

She ticked off his faults on her fingers, one by one. "Testy. Controlling. Rigid. Hypervigilant. I'd take no boundaries any day over brooding stick-in-the-mud."

"That's the worst you can do?" He arched an eyebrow, made come-on-let's-fight motions with his fingers.

"Oh," she said, new understanding dawning. "I finally get it."

"Get what?"

"You think you deserved to be punished. That's why you resist my attempts to draw you out. Sorry to break it to you, but I'm not going to be the one to crack the bullwhip against your back."

"Huh?" He made such a disgusted face that she knew she'd nailed him. Boone hadn't forgiven himself for coming home. Survivor's guilt. She didn't know much about the details of his injury, only snippets of local gossip, but clearly Boone was still torturing himself over it. Her heart went out to him.

Being a hairstylist gave her a peek into the human psyche. People spilled more confidences to her than to their therapists. There was something about having your hands deep in someone's hair that made them talky. An odd intimacy developed between a stylist and her clientele. A lack of conventional boundaries. It was one of the things she liked about her profession.

Boone's dark-eyed stare seared her skin, making her feel as naked as the day she was born. Things normally rolled right off her back, but for one split second she was tempted to jump into her car and drive away in the half-loaded U-Haul.

"We better get to work," she mumbled and reached for one of the boxes sitting on her kitchen table. "Without the movers this is going to take us twice as long."

He didn't say another word, just moved over to reach for a second box. In the process, his arm accidentally brushed against hers and a tingle of awareness shot straight to her groin. Instantly, her nipples tightened. *Hello, soldier, pleased to see you.*

Involuntarily, Tara sucked in her breath.

"What is it?" Boone asked. "Are you all right?"

"Just a catch in my back," she lied and set the box down.

"Where?"

She splayed a palm over her lower back, inched away from him. "It's all better. Gone already."

"Sounds like a muscle spasm." He came closer.

"I'm good." She'd never been able to get away with the occasional white lie—which was why she rarely told one. Falsehoods invariably came back to bite her in the butt.

He kept coming toward her. The closer he got, the more Tara's throat tightened. She would have kept backing up, but she was hemmed into the corner between the refrigerator and the stove.

"Let me see," he said.

"No need," she croaked.

He took her by the shoulders, slowly turned her around and didn't she just let him like some silly, awestruck teenager meeting her rock idol. His hands were warm and heavy, stirring up the languid sensation that had settled deep in her core.

"Here?" He rested his palm against her spine, just above the waistband of her shorts.

She swallowed, barely able to nod. Why was she nodding? The next thing she knew he was gently rubbing his knuckles across her back. He didn't say anything else, just kept slowly massaging her.

They stood like that for a while, not saying a word, Boone's big hand touching her so tenderly it suckerpunched her. The refrigerator cycled on with a click and hum. She could feel his slow, steady breathing stir her hair at her temple and this moment…the two of them in her kitchen together for the first and last time, was both strange and wondrous. And tainted with remorse, because it was too late now to start something up. They could have had something special, she and Boone. She felt it in her bones. If only she could have gotten him to walk across the street, open up his heart, months ago.

"How's that?" he asked, stepping back, leaving her both regretful and relieved.

"Fine, fine."

He scowled. "You shouldn't be lifting boxes."

She shifted her gaze to his knee. "Yes, Pot, are you calling the Kettle out?"

"You're right. I need to get some new movers in here ASAP."

"Or you could just call Rodney and Joe back and apologize."

He looked as if he'd rather have his leg squeezed in a vise. "Not a chance."

She sympathized. "Tell you what. I have a lot of friends. Let me give them a call. There's bound to be a few of them who wouldn't mind lending a hand."

He nodded with a quick jerk of his head. He had so much pride. This was really hard for him, letting others help him.

"Call 'em," he said gruffly and limped toward the back door.

Tara blew out her breath and pulled her cell phone from her pocket to start making calls. If she and Boone kept butting heads the entire way to Miami, it was shaping up to be a very long trip.

OVER A DOZEN of Tara's friends converged on the house. By the end of the afternoon, the U-Haul was packed and loaded, the house cleaned and empty of everything except the furniture that came with the rental. But now, everyone was sitting around drinking beer and eating the pizza that Tara had bought to thank them for their help. They were laughing and joking and lamenting about having to say goodbye. A few of her female friends even had tears in their eyes when they hugged her.

See, this was the problem with recruiting friends to help you move, Boone thought. You couldn't just pack up, say thanks for the help and get the hell out of town. No, you had to sit around and make small talk and linger. It wasn't worth the hassle.

Tara, however, was the life of her impromptu party. Teasing and smiling and telling everyone how much she appreciated their friendship. Promising to stay in touch via Facebook, Twitter and texts.

C'mon. All that social media stuff was crap. Nothing but a huge time suck. And honestly, those relationships were superficial at best. Why bother?

Yeah? These days, how many of your friends would show up to help you move?

Once upon a time, he'd had a handful of good friends he could count on, but these days? Boone licked his dry lips. Well, were they really friends? They'd abandoned him in tough times.

Or hey, maybe you were the one who pushed them away.

He caught Tara's eye from across the room and tapped the face of his watch. She gave him a bright, empty smile, like she thought he was the most pathetic guy in Bozeman.

Someone said something to her. She threw back her head and laughed with a rich, deep sound that rattled him to his core. No wonder people surrounded her like they were honeybees and she was their queen.

His gaze tracked from Tara's face down her long, slender throat to the cleavage revealed by the V-neck of her tie-dyed T-shirt. She had a cola in her hand. No beer for her, since she would be driving later tonight. His eyes dropped lower to take in those denim shorts sitting low on her curvy hips. The cuffed hem hit high on her thighs, showing off those pinup-quality legs.

He felt a stirring below his belt and swallowed hard. No, no. No way. She might be sexy as ten kinds of sin, but he was not even going to allow himself to fantasize about her. That was just inviting trouble. He had to be confined in a car with her for the next several days. He was not letting his libido off the chain. His focus was on getting to Key West to keep Jackie from making a huge mistake, and he was not going to let anything distract him.

Not even sexy Tara.

In fact, he was antsy as hell, hating that he had to wait for her to wind down this dumb party so they could get on the road. Plus, his leg was achy. He needed to get up and move around. He hoisted himself from the chair and limped toward the door.

The summer sun hung on the horizon. The evening breeze was cool against his face. Perfect. Just what he needed to snap him out of red-hot thoughts about Tara. He wasn't the kind of guy who went in for temporary flings, and of course that's all it could be between them. Not just because she was moving away, but because they had as much in common as a brightly colored helium balloon and a brick wall.

You're the brick wall.

That hadn't been a bad thing back in high school when he'd played linebacker. Or in the army where physical strength was a man's biggest asset. But now? The qualities he'd cultivated—staunchness, dependability, strength—were either lost to him or passé. What was a soldier without an enemy to vanquish?

"You're doing it again," a light voice murmured behind him.

Too close behind him. He could feel her body heat. Tara again. Violating boundaries. Hadn't she ever heard of personal space?

He stepped away from her and in his haste, almost lost his balance. If she hadn't reached out a hand to stabilize him, he would have taken a tumble off her porch. Damn knee. Damn heavy brace.

"Doing what?" he grumbled, wrenching his arm away. He caught a glimpse of her face in the shadows. For a split second she looked hurt, but quickly pasted a smile on her face.

You're a moron, Toliver.

"Brooding," she said.

"I'm not brooding. I just needed some air."

"Come back inside and have some pizza and beer," she invited, her voice soft and understanding.

She was so nice. Too damn nice. And ultimately, that was the real reason he would never ever sleep with her. He couldn't taint her happy little world. That's why he was gruff with her.

Well, she's moving now, all you have to do is get through the next few days and she'll be out of your life forever.

Why did that thought make his gut burn? He was glad she was going. No more having to make idle conversation with her. No more having to respond to her cheery conversations. No more Tara cluttering up his thoughts.

"We need to get on the road." He hitched his thumbs through his belt loops.

"Right." Her smile was wan. "You have a wedding to bust up."

"Jackie's making a big mistake."

"Because you know her so well." She was taunting him now, in that wide-eyed, "who, me?" way she had about her—all innocent, yet sly.

"She's my sister."

"And a grown woman."

"Are you saying I shouldn't try to protect her?"

"I'm saying that I understand how overprotective big brothers can be and how they can ruin a woman's love life when they stick their noses in where they don't belong. Why do you think I moved to Montana?"

"I thought you came up here after a cowboy."

"Yes, and my brothers hated him."

"From the way things turned out, seems like your brothers had a point."

Tara rolled her eyes. "Just because things didn't work out between me and Chet doesn't mean my brothers had the right to meddle in my business. The mistake was mine to make."

"And yet, you're running back home."

Her eyes flashed sparks. He'd upset her. He was good at that. Quite an accomplishment, since she was usually so easygoing.

"Because my mother is ill." She took a step toward him.

The smell of her—both sweet and sensual—tangled up in his nose. His body hardened instantly. He clenched his jaw to fight off the erection and prayed she would not look down.

"Is that the only reason?"

"I miss Florida. Nothing wrong with that."

"And your brothers. You miss them, too."

"I do," she admitted.

"I'm just saying, they probably have your best interests at heart. More so than some cowboy named Chet."

"I'll get rid of my friends," she said in a low voice that left him hungry and aroused.

His gaze hooked on her mouth. What beautiful, full lips, strawberry-pink and glistening with shiny gloss. "Thanks," he managed.

She touched him lightly, the bare brushing of her fingertips over his forearm, but it was enough to ignite his desire. He suppressed a groan.

"We'll be on the road within the hour." Tara turned and went back into the house.

Leaving Boone wondering how he was going to survive the next few days alone in a car with this tantalizing bombshell he wanted absolutely no part of.

3

FOR THE PAST three hours, they'd been driving east down lonely Highway 90. The barren landscape made Tara happy that she wasn't traveling this route alone. Montana was pretty, but in the dark, it stretched out long and lonesome.

Funny, she'd never noticed how empty the state was when she'd made the drive up from Florida fourteen months ago following Chet, more for fun and adventure than true love. Her friends raved about falling in love, finding that special someone, but Tara had never been that lucky. She'd liked lots of guys, sure, and had plenty of friends, but she'd never had that special connection with a guy.

Sometimes, she wondered if there was something wrong with her, some secret inability to experience love the way others did. Her mother told her it was simply because she just hadn't met the right man yet. The guy who would make her happy to give up her independence and settle down.

Tara sneaked a glance over at Boone and her heart

did this strange little tightening thing. She was grateful for Boone's company, even though he was trying mighty hard to pretend he was asleep.

The plan he'd given her—the control freak—detailed driving to Billings tonight, catching a few hours of sleep in a truck-stop motel and then hitting the road again at dawn. He'd programmed all their stops into his GPS and given her an estimated time frame for how long each stop should take. He'd made no allowances for detours. He was methodical and prepared. It drove Tara bonkers. How in the world could you truly experience life if you never strayed from the beaten path? If all your time was carefully plotted, where did spontaneity come in?

Boone had the passenger seat pushed back as far as it would go and he wore a Minnesota Twins baseball cap pulled down over his face. His breathing was slow and steady, but he had his arms crossed over his chest. Her gaze drifted down to his right leg encased in the metal brace. He had to be hurting from the day's efforts, but she hadn't seen him take a pain pill. He'd even refused the beer she'd offered him at her impromptu goodbye party.

Leaving Bozeman was more difficult than she'd thought it was going to be and it was all because of the man sitting beside her. She was excited about seeing her family again and happy that she wouldn't be spending another winter in Montana, but for all his gruffness, she was really going to miss Boone.

Her cell phone rang. Who was calling her this late at night? She couldn't see the caller ID in the dark, so she just answered it through the hands-free device that broadcast the conversation throughout the car. She tried to whisper so as not to disturb Boone. "Hello?"

"Tara? I can't hear you," said her older sister, Kate.

"I'm here." She raised her voice and cast a glance over at Boone to see if she was bothering him.

"Why are you calling so late? Is something wrong?"

"I'm at the hospital with Mom. She came through the surgery with flying colors and most likely she'll be released tomorrow."

Tara breathed out a sigh of relief. "That's good. I regret that I couldn't be there for the surgery."

"It's okay," Kate said. "You're coming home now."

"I'm sorry this is all falling on your shoulders."

"It's not. Everyone is pitching in. Joe and Matt are staying at the house with Dad. Erin and Dave are flying in tomorrow."

"I'm still several days away."

"No worries. You'll be home to help drive her to chemo treatments once she recovers from the surgery. Really, the doctors say she's got an excellent chance for a complete recovery."

"Still, it's scary to think of losing her."

"I know," Kate said softly. "She's really happy you're moving back home for good. We've all missed you."

Guilt nibbled at Tara. Her mother had been her biggest cheerleader, always urging her to follow her dreams and her heart, but she couldn't help feeling selfish that in her wanderlust, she'd left her family behind. While she loved adventure, Tara was a traditionalist at heart. Family meant a lot to her. It was time she went home.

"I'll call in the morning," Tara said.

"You be careful on the drive. Don't rush. We've got everything covered here."

More guilt. "'Night, Kate."

"Good night, Tara."

She cut off the call and peeped over at Boone again. Had he heard her conversation? The guilt turned into another feeling she couldn't quite identity, a cross between regret and wistfulness. He hadn't moved a muscle.

The car's headlights cut a swath through the darkness, the single illumination on the silent highway. A shiver of loneliness passed through her and, for a second, she felt as if she were completely alone on the surface of the moon.

Up ahead, she could see the lights of Billings, and an impish part of her wanted to drive on through without stopping. Throw off his best-laid plans; prove to him there was nothing wrong with a little impulsiveness. She would have done it, too, except she had no idea how far away the next town was.

"Take the next exit," Boone said.

Tara startled. "You're not even looking at the road. How do you know the exit to Billings is coming up next?"

"I have an acute sense of time. At the speed you're driving, we should be coming up to Billings."

She shifted her gaze to the clock in the dash. He was right on the money. "Dude, that's a freaky skill."

He shrugged, didn't bother to lift the cap off his face. There'd be no making end runs around this guy.

"Is the whole trip going to be like this?" she asked.

"Like what?"

"I'm only asking because if you're going to be quiet as a corpse the whole way, I want to dig out my earphones before we hit the road in the morning so I can listen to some tunes."

"You're not supposed to wear earbuds while you're driving."

"Yeah? Well, it's only common courtesy to have a conversation with the person who's driving you to

Miami. I mean it's miles and miles of driving. If you can't at least talk to me, then you're forcing me to break the law."

"You don't have to wear earbuds. You can play whatever you want on the radio."

"So, in other words, you're not going to talk to me."

He heaved a sigh, swept the cap from his face and sat up in the seat. "What do you want to talk about?"

"Nothing now. We're almost to the truck stop." She sailed up the exit ramp.

"Why don't you talk," he said. "Tell me something about yourself. Your hopes, your dreams, your secrets."

"Now you're making fun of me."

"Hey, you're the one who wanted to talk."

"You're impossible." Peeved, Tara reached over and clicked on the radio. The Black Keys were singing "Howlin' for You." She turned up the volume. Loud.

Boone winced.

"Too loud?" She smiled sweetly.

"No." He settled a hand on his knee.

"Is your knee hurting?" Contrite, she turned down the music.

"I don't need your pity. Crank the damn music." He reached over and turned the volume back up again.

"You're a real sorehead, you know that?"

"I wasn't always," he mumbled.

She wasn't sure she'd heard him correctly. She turned down the music. "What did you say?"

Silence settled over the car.

"I know you're a wounded warrior and all that, but this dark and broody stuff isn't working for me. Get some sleep tonight, but then tomorrow, I expect a complete attitude adjustment."

One eyebrow shot up high on his forehead. "Oh, you do?"

"I do." She pulled to a stop outside the bed-and-bath motel connected to the truck stop.

"You think it's that easy to just turn your mood around?"

"Fake it till you make it, baby." Okay, maybe she was being glib, but there was only so much gloom and doom she could handle and she'd noticed whenever she issued a challenge, he got feisty. "You know what I think?"

"How can anyone know what you think? Your mind jumps around like a spider monkey." The blinking lights of the motel sign flashed across his face in green neon.

Vacancy.

"I think that maybe deep down, underneath the pain and grief and pissiness, you're just plain bored."

"Bored, huh?"

"Yep. You're accustomed to lots of action and you're not getting any."

"Is that supposed to be a double entendre?" He lowered his eyelids, gave her a sultry look that sizzled her shorts.

Tara gulped, ignored that and trudged ahead. "From here on in, I want to see smiles, smiles, smiles."

"And if I don't?"

"I'll drive off and leave you."

"You wouldn't dare."

"Just try me."

He reached over and plucked the keys out of the ignition.

"Hey!"

"I'll give them back to you in the morning."

"You're a pain in the butt," she said. "Anyone ever tell you that?"

"All the time," he said. Then, for the first time that day, he gave her a genuine smile. "All the damn time."

EVEN IF BOONE didn't want to admit it, Tara was right. He was a pain in the butt, he was bored and he hadn't had any action in a very long time.

That included sex.

He lay on the narrow motel bed and stared up at the ceiling. He could hear the chuff of Jake brakes as eighteen-wheelers rolled in off the highway. He tried to sleep, but Tara crowded and clouded his mind. He had underestimated exactly how tough this was going to be—sitting beside her in the car, hour after hour, smelling her feminine scent, taking in the bare stretch of skin from the hem of her shorts to her sandals, hearing the sweet sound of her voice. It was all he could do to keep his hands off her. Now, he fully realized why he'd kept her at arm's length all these months.

She was in the room next door. The walls were thin and when she'd taken her shower, he heard the water come on.

Instantly, he pictured her in those shorts that crept high on her thighs when she sat down. She had million-dollar legs and he imagined her sliding them over his. Her features were etched on the back of his eyelids and it was as real as if she were standing right in front of him—from the gentle arch of her sandy eyebrows to her determined little chin beneath those wide, luscious lips. Her face was shaped like a soft heart, wider across the forehead, smaller at her jawline. Her nose was short with a delicate tip.

He might want to deny it, but she was cuter than a basketful of puppies. Boone hated cute. Nothing could trip a guy up faster than cute.

An unwelcome stiffness gripped him.

Dammit. He did not want her starring in his X-rated fantasies, but his body had other ideas, his brain teasing his appendage with provocative images of her. Stepping out of the shower, naked, wet and slippery.

She turned him inside out and she wasn't even in the same room.

"Stop thinking about her," he commanded himself, but it was like telling a dieter to stay away from chocolate cake.

Goose bumps spread over him at the thought of what it would feel like to take her into his arms with those spectacular breasts pressed against his chest. Inhale the scent of her hair. Taste the sweetness of her lips.

His erection tightened, throbbed.

Ah, hell.

He flopped ungracefully over onto his side, dragging his injured knee after him and stared at the digital clock on the bedside table. Two in the morning. He was never going to get any sleep at this rate.

His shaft ached. He pulled in a deep breath.

Just do it and get it over with so you can get a few hours of sleep.

He didn't want to give in. His body had betrayed him enough, but if he didn't do something about this erection soon, he'd lie awake until dawn.

Once upon a time, he'd had an iron will, but these days? No such luck.

The persistent throbbing won out. Blowing out his breath, Boone reached down a hand, and with visions of Tara parading through his head, proceeded to take care of his problem in the most expedient way possible.

SUNLIGHT PUSHING through the dusty window jerked Boone awake sometime later. He sat up abruptly and immediately regretted it when his knee twinged. He gritted his teeth, shoved a hand through his hair. What in the hell time was it? His plan had been to get on the road at dawn. What he'd done last night had worked, but he'd slept far longer than he intended.

A glance over at the clock told him it was seven-thirty—a good hour and a half later than he'd planned. He'd no sooner gotten dressed and put on his knee brace than a knock sounded at his door. He opened it to find Tara standing there wearing a short red sundress and matching red sandals that showed off the sexiest toes this side of Montana.

"Good morning," she chirped.

"Why did you let me sleep so long?" he groused. "I told you we needed to be on the road by six."

"Relax. We've got plenty of time. You don't have to be in Key West until Saturday."

"It's already Wednesday and I don't like cutting things close."

"C'mon." She beckoned with a wriggly finger. "Let's go have breakfast."

"No. Let's get on the road. We can hit a drive-through on the way out of town."

But she was already swishing away from him, headed across the parking lot toward the truck-stop diner, her oversized purse slung over her shoulder.

He swore under his breath, picked up his knapsack and limped after her as fast as he could. "Tara," he hollered. "We don't have time for this."

Stepping lightly, she turned and, still walking toward the diner, grinned at him. "You'll feel better after a hearty breakfast."

"I'll feel better when we're on the road."

"Breakfast is the most important meal of the day."

"Watch where you're walking."

"I'm—" Her retort was cut off by an eighteen-wheeler bread truck as it whizzed away from massive gas pumps at the back of the diner. The truck came barreling straight for Tara.

Adrenaline shot through Boone. His natural instinct was to run toward her, throw himself between her and the truck, but given the shape his knee was in, he simply could not move that fast. "Stop!" he commanded and then took half a dozen deities' names in vain.

Tara froze, her face gone deathly pale.

The driver of the eighteen-wheeler blasted his horn, coming within inches of Tara as he rocketed from the parking lot.

Boone's stomach had vaulted into his throat.

She jumped then, leaping into a hedge of bushes surrounding the diner. Boone moved as fast as he could, heart hammering. He'd intended to give her a good long lecture, but when he reached her, she was trembling all over.

"Are you all right?" he murmured.

She nodded mutely. Her legs wobbled beneath her.

He reached out and took her into his arms.

"You were right," she said. "We should have gotten on the road. If we'd been on the road ahead of that stupid truck, I wouldn't have been acting like a dummy."

"Shh, it's okay. You're safe," he reassured her, but she was a leaf in his arms, shaking uncontrollably.

"That was almost the end of me. Why don't I ever think?"

"You were just caught up in the moment, enjoying the morning. There's nothing wrong with that."

"It could have been my last breath." She leaned heavily against him.

"Maybe you shouldn't have been walking backward," he conceded. "But that guy shouldn't have come cannonballing around the building knowing that people come walking through the parking lot from the motel to the diner."

"You're letting me off the hook?" She seemed surprised.

"I think you're shaken up enough without me making any more comments. Let's get some breakfast," he murmured in her ear, surprised by the tender feeling of relief that had evaporated all his anger. She was okay. That's all that mattered.

"No, we should get on the road."

"You're in no shape to drive. You need to sit down a bit. Get some color back into those cheeks."

"Okay," she agreed in a weak voice.

Boone let his hand drop to her waist, pressed his palm to the small of her back and escorted her toward the door. He had the strangest urge to grin.

They found a booth near the front door. Tara plunked down. It took Boone a minute to get seated across from her. He dropped his knapsack to the floor and stretched his right leg out across it.

Tara exhaled audibly.

He reached across the table to touch her hand. "You sure you're okay?"

Her smile was wan. She pushed a lock of hair from her eyes. "I'm getting there."

The waitress came over. Boone ordered oatmeal and toast. Tara ordered the Slam Bang special. He eyed her speculatively. Where did she plan on putting all that food?

"What?" she asked as she handed the waitress her menu.

"I didn't say anything."

"I have a high metabolism. I can eat like a horse and not gain weight."

"Good for you."

She took a sip of the orange juice the server brought her but didn't meet his gaze. The steam from Boone's coffee curled up between them. She fiddled with the wrapper from her straw, rolling the paper around her index finger, then unfurling it again.

"So," she said. "How do you plan to get back home after you ruin your sister's wedding?"

Boone blinked at her. For all his planning out the route and time scheduled, it had never once crossed his mind how he was going to get back to Montana. He'd been so single-minded about reaching Key West in time to stop Jackie from making a big mistake that he'd forgotten the return trip home.

"I'll figure something out," he said.

"Wow, something the great planner hasn't thought out? I'm shocked."

"Yeah, well, I was preoccupied."

"Sticking your nose in your sister's business."

"It's not like that."

"No?" She planted her elbows on the table, rested her chin into her upturned palms. "What's it like?"

"This is the first time Jackie has ever been in love. She doesn't understand that she can't trust those feelings."

"Why not?"

"They're not based on anything solid." He studied her mouth. "It's just lust. Not the real thing. You should know that."

"What does that mean?"

"Guys fall all over you."

"So?" She narrowed her eyes. "You think I've been in love gobs of times?"

"Haven't you?"

"Just because I'm lively and like people doesn't mean I go falling in love willy-nilly."

That was precisely what he'd thought of her. Her house was always filled with people. She dated a lot. It was a natural assumption.

"How many times have you been in love?" he asked, not knowing why he was pursuing this topic. It was none of his damned business.

She studied him for a long moment, her winsome blue eyes drilling into his until he started feeling downright antsy. "How many times have *you* been in love?"

Boone drummed his fingers on the Formica tabletop. "I asked you first."

She dropped her hands into her lap, notched up her chin. "I don't think I've ever been in love."

"Not even with Chet?"

"Oh, heck no. He was good in bed and lots of fun and I was ready for an adventure. I was going through a cowboy phase, which was why I moved up here with him."

Jealousy shot through Boone, crisp and concise. The last thing he wanted to think about was Tara in bed with that cowboy. He wondered if she'd ever gone through a soldier phase, and then mentally kicked himself for wondering it.

"So you weren't crushed when he left?"

"Only because I had to pay the rent all on my own." Boone shook his head.

"What?" A smile played at her lips.

"I envy you."

"For what?"

"The easy way you take life."

"So you *have* been in love." She nodded as if he'd just confirmed something she suspected.

"I thought I was, once. That's how I know what love is not."

Tara leaned forward, rubbed her palms together. "Ooh, now it's getting juicy. What was her name?"

"I don't want to talk about it."

"Still hung up on her, huh?"

"No, not at all. I'm just embarrassed that I let her make a fool of me."

"She cheated on you."

"Yeah." He bit off the word, grateful to see the waitress coming toward them with their breakfast.

"Well," Tara said, "at least you're not commitment-phobic."

"Are you?"

She wrinkled her nose. "Kinda. Sorta. At least that's what Chet said."

"I thought he was the one who left you."

"Yeah, when I turned down his marriage proposal."

"Poor Chet," Boone said, not feeling sorry for ol' Chet in the least. "You broke his heart."

She shrugged. "Not on purpose. I was very clear from the beginning that it wasn't a long-term relationship."

"Are you always that clear about your expectations from a relationship?"

"Aren't you?"

"No," he admitted.

She dug into her breakfast, fork in one hand, knife in the other, both elbows sticking out. The platter was heaped high with bacon and eggs and pancakes and hash browns. "You want some? I got plenty."

He raised a palm. "I'm good."

She narrowed her eyes at his oatmeal. "That's not enough to feed a sparrow."

"Since I'm not mobile, I have to keep a check on the calorie count."

"Suit yourself." She waved a fork. "So what was her name?"

"Who?"

"The one who broke your heart."

He shrugged.

"You forgot her name?"

"Believe me, I wanted to."

"Isn't it a shame we can't get selective amnesia when it suits us."

"Shame," he echoed.

"So what was her name?"

"Does it matter?"

"Not to me, but maybe if you talked about her, you could get over her."

"I'm over her."

"You sure?" She sank her teeth into a sausage link.

"Positive."

"Then tell me her name."

"Shaina."

"Pretty name. Was she good in bed?"

"Excuse me?"

"It's a legitimate question. The top two reasons couples break up are money and sex."

Boone couldn't believe she was asking something so personal. Then again, he could. Tara had no boundaries. Was it strange that, while her questions rubbed him the wrong way, he was starting to admire the way she just said whatever popped into her head? No filter. No caution. Just plowing straight ahead and grabbing at life with open arms. Trouble was, he was a cactus and she was a shiny red balloon.

"It wasn't money," he growled.

"So she *was* bad in bed." Tara wiped her fingers on a napkin. "Could you hand me the syrup?"

He passed the syrup. "No, she was very good in bed. Everyone's bed. That was the problem. Her extreme proficiency in bed."

Tara's eyes went all goopy soft as she drizzled maple syrup over her pancakes. "Oh, Boone, I'm so sorry."

"Why? Did you sleep with her?"

Her hearty laugh captured him. Embraced him like a hug. How could someone hug you with a laugh?

A man put money in the jukebox and at eight o'clock in the morning, with the smell of bacon wafting in the air, it was downright incongruous hearing Ingrid Michaelson singing "Be OK."

"That's really why you want to stop Jackie from getting married, isn't it?" Tara surprised him with her chirpy insight. "To keep her from making the same mistake you did. It's really your mistakes you want to erase, not hers."

Boone shook his head, polished off his oatmeal. "She barely knows the guy. They've only been going out a few weeks."

"You and your sister weren't raised together, right?"

"Yes. Where'd you hear that?"

"When I said goodbye to Mrs. Levison at the party, she said your sister is the daughter of Jack Birchard, the famous oceanographer."

"That's right. She's my half sister."

"Why the deep investment? It takes a lot of time, money and energy to drive across the country to ruin someone's wedding."

"I wasn't there for her when she was growing up."

"Why do you feel that it was your responsibility to be there for her?"

"When our mom dumped her, I could have made things easier for her."

"Don't flatter yourself. A big brother can't make up for an AWOL mother."

"I could have told her it wasn't her fault that she left."

"I doubt you telling her that would have made a difference."

"Yeah, well."

"You still feel guilty even when it had nothing to do with you. C'mon, Boone, you're not responsible for what your mother did. I'm sure Jackie doesn't hold you accountable in any way."

This was making him uncomfortable. This is what he got for opening up to her. She was kicking off her shoes, climbing into his brain, making herself right at home, running barefoot through his psyche. He folded his arms over his chest. "You sure take your time over a meal."

"You're supposed to eat slowly. It aids digestion."

"It does not aid expediency."

"You went to college," she said.

"I did."

"You use a lot of big words."

"In some circles, a large vocabulary is considered an asset."

"I didn't go," she said, wistfully licking syrup from her fork. "To college, that is. My parents couldn't afford it. Not on a plumber and secretary's salary. Too many kids. I put myself through beauty school."

"Doing what?"

"Swear you won't laugh."

"What? Did you work in a strip club?"

"Boone!" She looked half amused, half insulted. "What in the world do you think of me?"

He raked a gaze over her. "With a body like that you could make a fortune dancing."

Her cheeks pinked and she looked both pleased and embarrassed. "Thank you. I think. No, I worked at an amusement park."

"Doing what?"

"I was a character."

"You are that."

She rolled her eyes. "Specifically, a chipmunk."

"You got the spunk of a chipmunk. I'll give you that."

"Why, thank you. That's exactly what they told me at Florida Land."

"You finished?" He tapped the face of his watch. "It's almost nine. We've got to hit the road."

"You know, if you keep doing that I'm gonna have to smash that watch."

He narrowed his eyes, pretended to be affronted when he wasn't. "You wouldn't dare."

"It's for your own good." She bit into a crisp slice of bacon, her gaze hooked on his. "You don't know how to slow down, relax and take it easy."

"I've had plenty of time to sit around. It drives me batty. Relaxing is severely overrated."

"Because your mindset is rush, rush, rush, go, go, go. It's killing you to be incapacitated. That's why you had to go back for a third surgery. Because you couldn't sit still and just be. Now you're having to learn the hard way that life doesn't always turn out the way you planned."

"How much do I owe you for the analysis, Dr. Freud?"

Tara grinned. "It's on the house."

"And the advice is well worth every penny."

"Oh-ho, here come the barbs."

"I wanted to be on the road hours ago."

"And here we were getting along so well there for a split second."

"You'd think you'd be in a hurry, too," Boone said. "To see your mother."

A shadow flickered over her face. "I'm not very good when those I love are sick."

"But you're going home anyway."

"Of course. I love my mother."

"Yet here you are, over a thousand miles away."

She shifted uncomfortably. "It was my mom who told me to follow my bliss. She encouraged me to leave Florida."

"Why's that?"

"She got married young and started having kids, and even though she never said it, I think she regretted not getting to have adventures."

"What did your dad say?"

"He's my dad. He was dead set against it, but Mom convinced him."

"Could you get a to-go bag for the rest of that?" He nodded at her half-eaten breakfast.

The waitress led a cowboy past their table. Boone pointed at Tara's plate, silently mouthed "to-go box" to the waitress and pantomimed signing the check.

The waitress nodded.

"I90 East is a mess," the cowboy told the waitress. "Eighteen-wheeler jackknifed and turned over, blocked that entire side of the freeway. Bread truck. Loaves of bread and buns strewn everywhere. You should have seen the birds flocking. I thought I was in a Hitchcock movie."

Tara tucked her legs underneath her, sat up higher in her seat, looked over Boone's head to the cowboy in the booth behind him. "Excuse me, sir."

"Yes, ma'am," the cowboy said.

"Did you say a bread truck overturned on the freeway?"

"Yep. Traffic is backed up all the way from here to the state line. It'll be hours before they get that mess untangled. If you're headed that direction, stay on the access road."

"Thank you." She threw the cowboy a beaming smile, then slipped her feet back on the floor and was back eye-to-eye with Boone. "You owe me an apology," she said.

"How do you figure?"

"If we'd been on the road like you wanted, we'd be trapped in traffic with no way out. In fact, we probably would have been right behind that bread truck. It might have turned over on us. Squashed us flat."

"You have a very active imagination," Boone said because there was no way he was going to admit she was right. It was one thing to put up with her Mary Sunshine attitude. It was quite another to give her a reason to gloat.

She gloated anyway. "And the moral of that story, Toliver, is that sometimes it's better to be the tortoise than the hare."

4

TARA HAD A MISSION. Cheer Boone up. Whenever he smiled, he dazzled, and when he laughed, well, she melted, gooey as chocolate in the hot sun. Unfortunately, he rarely laughed.

Why do you care? He's not your problem. He's not a project and you're not chocolate.

No, but she was stuck in the car with him and she preferred sunshine to rain. They'd been driving for hours and they were almost out of Nebraska. Once they'd left the truck stop, taking an alternate route that the cowboy had suggested to avoid the bread truck smashup on the freeway, they'd made great time.

She slid a glance over at Boone. He was staring out the window at the Nebraska cornfields rolling by. His clenched fist rested on his right leg.

"Are you hurting?"

"What?" He blinked, turned to meet her gaze.

"Your leg. Do you need some pain pills?"

"It's fine. I'll live. I'm trying to taper off."

"You don't have to suffer. If you need a pill, take it."

He shook his head. "I've been taking the easy way out. This thing with Jackie woke me up. I can't keep stewing in pills and self-pity."

"It's only been three weeks since your last surgery. You're still healing."

He grunted. "Or maybe this is as good as it gets."

Tara didn't know what to say to that. She knew he was going to get better, but from his point of view things had to look a little dark right now. "I broke my leg once."

He raised an eyebrow.

"When I was eleven."

"How'd it happen?"

"Stilts accident."

"Stilts?" An amused smile flitted at the corners of his mouth. "Now that's unusual."

"My brother Matt is a powerbocker."

"A power what?"

"It's an extreme sport where you jump and run on spring-loaded stilts, but that's not the kind I fell off of. Matt experimented with all kinds of stilts before he discovered powerbocking."

"Is he short?"

"Who? My brother? Yeah, kinda. Five foot six."

"What kind of stilts did you fall off of?"

"Peg stilts."

"What are peg stilts?"

"They're also called Chinese stilts and are used by professional performers. On peg stilts you have to keep walking at all times in order to keep yourself from falling over."

"No stopping, huh?"

"None."

"Can't stay in one place?"

"Nope."

"How in the world do you dismount?"

"Therein lies the challenge that I was working on when Matt caught me and hollered. I started running to get away from him. Not smart. Seriously, do not run on peg stilts."

"I'll take that into consideration the next time I'm stilt walking. What happened next?"

"I stepped on some boggy ground—we've got a lot of that in Florida—and one of the stilts got stuck. I did the splits midair."

"Ouch." Sympathy tinged his voice.

She winced in memory. "It was not a pretty sight."

"How long were you in a cast?"

"Six weeks. But shh, it was sort of humorous after I got past the initial pain. I didn't have to do dishes and I got to be the center of attention, which is very important to the middle child in a family with six kids. I milked it for all it was worth."

"Ah," he said. "You're one of those lemonade people."

"Pardon?"

"Life gives you lemons, yada, yada."

"There's nothing wrong with lemonade."

"I wish I could have seen you walking on stilts," he mused, his voice softening. "Not when you fell, of course. I wouldn't want to see you get hurt."

"Really?" She canted her head, studied him.

"Just…well…you're so graceful. I bet when you walked on stilts it was like you were dusting clouds."

"Why, Boone, how romantic. That's the nicest thing anyone has ever said to me."

He made a face. "Really? As I was saying it, I thought, 'Come on, Toliver, this is way too cheesy.'"

"It might have sounded cheesy coming from someone else, but you do not throw around compliments, so when you say something like that, I know you mean it."

A long silence stretched between them and Tara started fretting that she'd said too much.

"I don't dislike you, you know," he mumbled.

Her heart thumped strangely. "You don't?"

"Not at all."

"You're not very friendly to me most of the time."

"It's because you scare the hell out of me."

"I do?"

"Yeah."

Tara gulped past the odd lump in her throat. "Why's that?"

"Because I do like you."

"Really?"

"That's the problem," he rushed to add. "I don't want to like you."

She felt a little hurt that he didn't want to like her, but she pretended it rolled right off her shoulders. "Any particular reason why?"

"You're hard to keep up with."

"What does that mean?"

"You've got a quicksilver mind."

"Is that a compliment or a complaint?"

"Just an observation."

"What does quicksilver mean, exactly?"

"Changing unpredictably."

"I don't do that."

"You do," he disagreed.

"Oh, look." She pointed at the red sports car that sped by them in the fast lane. "A Porsche Boxster. I always wanted one of those."

"If you were in school these days they'd probably diagnose you with ADHD and put you on Ritalin."

Tara pursed her lips in thought. "Probably. I took home all kinds of notes telling my parents I was a chatterbox who couldn't sit still."

That got a smile from him. It was small, but it was a smile and damn if she didn't feel pleased as punch. "Some things never change."

"Let me guess what kinds of notes you took home from school." Tara tapped her index finger against her chin. "'Dear Mr. Toliver, Boone dusts the erasers far too hard when he's playing teacher's pet.'"

"I didn't get notes in school."

Tara laughed. "Why am I not the least bit surprised?"

"You know," he said, "this isn't so bad."

"What isn't?"

"Being trapped in a car with you."

"You thought it was going to be bad?"

"Well, yeah," he admitted. "I mean, we don't get along at the best of times and a cross-country road trip is definitely not the best of times."

"What do you mean, we don't get along? I thought we got along famously."

"You did?"

"Sure."

"Lemonade," he mumbled.

"I know you don't really mean it when you get all grumbly. You just don't want anyone seeing you with your guard down so you push people away. I don't take it personally."

"You forgive everyone." He sounded amazed. "Do you take *anything* personally?"

"Meredith Moncu," she said.

Boone frowned. "I'm not following."

"Meredith Moncu. I took her personally."

"Who is Meredith Moncu?"

"My high school rival. She was always beating me out for everything. Head cheerleader—"

"You were a cheerleader?"

"Hustle! Get to it! Gators, let's do it!" Tara cheered.

Boone groaned good-naturedly. "I had to ask."

"Get fired up! Let's go! Have at it! Let's roll!" She clapped and pantomimed raised pompoms over her head.

"Hands on the wheel, Duvall." He grabbed for the steering wheel.

She warded him off with her elbow. "I've got it under control. Settle down."

"Not my strong suit."

"What? Letting go of control?"

"Yeah."

"You should work on that."

"What else did Meredith Moncu beat you out of?"

"Class president."

"High school politics? Seriously, you dodged a bullet."

"She also stole my first boyfriend. Bobby Joe Harding."

"Bobby Joe? Sounds like you dodged a bullet there, too."

"He had a lot of muscles." She turned her head to assess Boone's biceps. "But you could have taken him in arm wrestling."

"Good to know. Whatever happened to Bobby Joe?"

"Oh, he knocked Meredith up and they got married. They have four kids now and live in Buena Vista trailer park down by the railroad tracks."

"See, you *did* dodge a bullet."

She shook her head. "I wouldn't have gotten pregnant."

"Knew a lot about birth control, did you?"

"Nope. I didn't put out. Which is how Meredith stole him."

"Really?"

"What part? Meredith putting out, or me not putting out?"

"You."

"Don't sound shocked. What? You think I'm Suzie Sleep Around?"

"I never said that."

"You didn't have to. Your face did." She shrugged. "I just wasn't ready for sex when I was in high school. I wanted to be in love and I wasn't in love with Bobby Joe."

"I thought you said you'd never been in love before. If you've never been in love, does that mean…"

"I'm not a virgin, if that's what you're asking. Cripes, Boone, I'm twenty-five. After a while…well…a girl has certain needs and her lofty ideals fall by the wayside."

"I suppose they do," he said, his voice turning husky.

"I'm old-fashioned, really."

"You?" Boone hooted. "In what way are you old-fashioned?"

"I believe in marriage, for one thing."

"Me, too."

"Even though you've been divorced? Even though your mom flaked out on your dad?"

"Even though. What else do you believe in?"

"Waiting until you get married before you have a baby. For me, I mean. I wouldn't presume to tell other people how to make their choices."

The car tires strummed along the asphalt.

"You're not quite what I thought you were," Boone said after a while.

"The flakey hairstylist syndrome, huh?"

"What's that?"

"When people hear you're a hairstylist they assume certain things about you. That you're arty and creative and impulsive and undependable and have scads of tattoos."

"And you're not those things?"

She notched up her chin. "I'm dependable."

"Do you have any more tattoos? I mean, besides the dolphin."

She felt the heat of his gaze roll over her. "Would you be disappointed or relieved if I said no?"

He shrugged, didn't answer. Silence filled the car. Tara sneaked another glance over at Boone. He was studying her with a pensive expression on his face, as if she were as mysterious to him as a platypus.

"How come you don't date?" she asked.

"With this?" He waved a hand at his knee.

"You're using that as an excuse."

"That's because it *is* an excuse. Can't perform bedroom gymnastics in a metal leg brace."

"Have you ever tried?"

"No, I haven't tried."

"Then how do you know what you can't do?"

"Because—"

"I get it. Performance anxiety. You're afraid of rejection."

"I'm not afraid of rejection." He snorted.

"You know, if you had a girlfriend, you might not be so jealous of your sister Jackie's happiness."

"I'm not jealous of Jackie's happiness!" he growled.

"Um, yeah, okay."

"I'm not!"

"You're traveling three thousand miles with a former cheerleader who makes you uncomfortable in a Honda Accord pulling a U-Haul trailer just to stop Jackie from marrying the man she's madly in love with."

"You don't make me uncomfortable."

That gave Tara pause. She was glad she had a reason to keep her eyes straight ahead, but she could feel the heat of his stare. "You don't have to be polite. If you don't dislike me as you claim, how come you never came to my parties?"

"I'm not a party guy."

"How come you shut your curtains when you see me coming across the street to your house?"

"I'm not good company."

"How come you won't ask me to drive you to the doctor or the grocery store? And don't say pride, because I know you've let some of the other neighbors help you."

"Because I have nothing to offer you," he said so faintly she wasn't sure she heard him.

She moistened her lips. The tension in the car stretched tight. His breathing was rough. Her breathing was none too smooth either. "I didn't want anything from you other than to be a good neighbor. It's not like I wanted to jump your bones or anything."

"Yeah?" he said. "Well, maybe I wanted you to."

WHY THE HELL had he told Tara that?

Her sharp inhalation filled the car. "You…you want to jump my bones?"

"I wouldn't put it so crudely, but yeah, I've had a fantasy or two about you." *Shut up! Just shut your damn mouth right now. Don't say another freaking word.*

"*Real*-ly?" She sounded pleased. "I've had a fantasy or two about you, too."

Boone felt as uncomfortable as a woolly sheep in a Swedish sauna. His body tightened in all the wrong places. Or all the right places. Depending on how you looked at it.

He moistened his lips. Traffic was slowing. Up ahead he could see a flashing roadside sign with an arrow indicating they should merge left.

"What's going on?" he asked.

"Well," Tara said breezily, "I think we're admitting to a mutual attraction."

"Not that. The road."

"Oh." She shifted her attention to the road and then glanced into the rearview mirror. She flicked on the turn signal and started edging over to the far lane. "Looks like we've run into some roadwork."

"Dammit," Boone swore under his breath, secretly grateful to have an excuse to get out of their conversation.

Traffic slowed to a crawl and then stopped altogether.

Boone shifted in his seat. His knee was achy—when wasn't it?—and every muscle in his body was wound tense. He'd known that the drive to Florida with Tara would be a challenge. What he hadn't expected was to turn into a damn chatterbox, confessing stuff he had no business confessing to her. His plan had been to keep his trap shut and simply endure. He'd shot that all to hell.

Tara hummed tunelessly, drumming her fingers on the dashboard. Long, slender fingers with nails painted the color of Pacific salmon. Bright and eye-catching, just like the woman wearing it.

Boone slid a melted-butter gaze over her, slippery and hot. He couldn't believe how much she rattled him with that beguiling smile of hers and that chirpy go-getter attitude. She had the body of a professional dancer and she smelled like a strawberry patch—all ripe and juicy. Why did she have to be so damn appealing?

Stop thinking about her. It's not like you can act on the attraction. No bedroom activities for you. Not with that bum leg. While you're at it, stop staring at her.

He shifted his gaze out the side window, saw rows and rows of cornfields. Nothing in the scenery to distract him.

Think about Jackie. She's the reason you're here. You've got to make it to Key West before she marries that coastie.

It had been a while since he'd tried to call his little sister. Maybe she'd relented and turned on her voice mail. Maybe she'd come to her senses and realized getting married to someone she barely knew was a huge mistake. Resolutely ignoring Tara, who was stretching the kinks from her neck muscles, Boone took his cell phone from his front pocket and punched in Jackie's number.

It rang and rang and rang. No voice mail picked up. Finally, after the twentieth ring, he hung up. His sister must still be royally ticked off at him. With a growl, he switched off the phone and stuck it back into his pocket.

They hadn't moved an inch in the traffic jam. They were behind a white Chevy pickup truck loaded down with a small cement mixer. Tara had her left elbow propped on the door frame, the left side of her head resting in the open palm of her hand. She was still humming.

"Snow on a shingle," Boone grumbled. "This is ridiculous. How long have we been sitting here?"

"Chill, dude. It's only been five minutes."

"Of not moving one inch. What are they doing up there? Rebuilding the entire freeway?"

"There's nothing we can do about it. Might as well make the most of a bad situation. Wanna play a game? I spy with my little eye—"

"No, I don't want to play a game. I want to drive. I want to get the hell to Key West. I want to sit down with my sister, face-to-face, and convince her to call off this crazy wedding."

"Something red."

"Marriage isn't something to take lightly. It's not a lark. It's a commitment. You shouldn't go into it thinking it's going to be all pancakes and morning sex, because it's not."

"I spy something red and very close."

"Divorce is painful and costly."

"I spy—"

"I'm not playing the dumb game! It's for children," Boone roared, louder and more harshly than he'd intended. He wasn't mad at Tara. He wasn't even mad at Jackie. He was mad at himself. For not being there for his sister. For getting injured. For not taking care of himself properly and having to have more surgeries. For losing control. That's what angered him most. How he'd lost control over his own life.

"Why not?" she asked calmly. "You're acting like a big baby. You don't get your way and you pitch a fit. I told you it's not a good idea to travel when Mercury is in retrograde."

"And you're acting like a total fruitcake." Boone snorted. "Mercury in retrograde. What a load of horse manure."

"Horse manure, huh? What about the bread truck accident we narrowly missed? And now a big construction holdup. Mercury. Retrograde. It's a thing. Look it up."

"It's coincidence. It's got nothing to do with planetary misalignment. That's nonsensical thinking."

"And you're the last word on what's nonsense?"

"In this case, yes."

"You're getting yourself worked up over nothing."

"It's not nothing. Each detour is taking me farther away from my sister."

"I don't think distance is the only obstacle between you and your sister."

"No?"

"The crux of the problem could be your sanctimonious attitude. Believe it or not, Boone, you don't have all the answers."

"Yeah? Well, you ignore the damn questions. You stick your head in the sand, pretending the world is a good place."

"The world *is* a good place."

"Wearing rose-colored glasses doesn't change reality."

"What would you have me do?" she exclaimed. "Sit on my porch and glare at everyone for the mess the world is in? Dwelling on problems and difficulties doesn't make the world a better place. Bitching and griping doesn't improve things. My positive outlook might not feed a starving child in the Congo, but it damn well makes my world a better place to live in. I light up people's lives, that's more than you can claim, Toliver." She stared straight ahead, hands gripping the wheel, her chin quivering slightly.

Friggin' hell, he'd hurt her feelings. Okay. He was a jerk. He admitted it. Why had he taken his anger out on her? She was an innocent bystander and he'd lashed out at the nearest person.

Well, what did she expect? He'd tried to warn her

off. He was damaged. Couldn't she see how messed up he was? Why did she try so hard to salvage him? He didn't deserve her attempts. Why had he bitten her head off? He hadn't wanted to hurt her. In fact, he'd wanted to do the exact opposite. Pull her into his arms. Kiss her until neither one of them could stop. He was a control freak know-it-all whose world had been knocked topsy-turvy. He was a lost cause and he resented her trying to save him.

"Sitting there spouting happy-happy, joy-joy mantras isn't going to get us to Miami any faster," he mumbled, ashamed but not knowing how to back down.

Tara jerked her head in his direction, flames flashing in her eyes. "You want out of this traffic jam?"

"Yes. Yes, I do."

"Fine." Tara set her determined little chin and whipped the steering wheel hard to the left. The Honda hopped onto the grass median, the U-Haul creaking and groaning behind them.

"What *are* you doing?"

"Making everything right in Boone's dark world." She jammed her foot down hard on the accelerator.

The Honda rocketed forward.

Boone grabbed the grip strap, clenched it in his fist. "You're gonna get the cops after us. You're gonna bust an axle. You're gonna—"

"If you can't say something productive, shut up!" Tara yelled, struggling to control the car.

Shocked, Boone clamped his mouth shut. They bounced and jostled over the uneven terrain. Cars honked at them. Tara's gaze was fixed straight ahead. He had visions of the U-Haul getting stuck in the median, but miraculously, she traversed it and joined the flow of traffic headed in the opposite direction.

She changed lanes, easing over and taking the next exit.

He started to ask where she was going, but decided against it. He was afraid of what she might do next. She was quicksilver, unpredictable, and damn if that didn't excite him.

At the intersection, which in Nowhere, Nebraska, consisted of nothing more than a two-way stop sign, she went back the direction they'd been traveling, but instead of merging onto the freeway, she took off down a one-lane dirt road that ran through the cornfields. She sped along, dust billowing out behind them.

"Happy now?" She glared.

"Tara—"

She raised a palm. "I don't want to hear about it, Boone. You got what you wanted. We're no longer stuck in traffic and we're headed south to Miami."

"Tara—"

"No, I'm not going to listen. I know what you're going to say. I'm an airhead, a flake. It was a very stupid thing, jumping the median. I probably broke a dozen laws. I'm sure I screwed up something on the U-Haul and that'll cost money, but you are on your way. You got what you wanted. So be happy. I don't want to hear whatever criticism you've got loaded up for me."

"Tara," he insisted softly.

She heaved a big sigh and for the first time since she broke ranks from the traffic jam, she switched her attention to meet his eyes. "What? Just what the hell is it, Boone?"

"I'm sorry."

5

WELL, BOONE'S APOLOGY was unexpected. She hadn't known the man was capable of remorse.

"And thank you," he added.

She eyed him suspiciously. He didn't look like he was being sarcastic. Still, he had the power to crush her to dust with his biting commentary, so she didn't trust his earnest tone.

"I was acting like a tool."

"Yes, you were. A right contentious hammer. Bam, bam, bamming me flat as an innocent nail."

"I could blame it on my military training, but I won't."

"Contrite *and* taking responsibility? I guess this means I have to forgive you," she answered, softening already.

She was so easy. She had every right to stay mad at him, but the truth was she hated hanging on to resentment. It was so much easier to forgive than pout.

"You're right," he conceded. "I do have control issues."

She fake-gasped. "Shocker."

His lips pulled straight back in a wry smile. "The army psychologist said it was because my mother abandoned me, but I don't believe in that blame-it-all-on-your-mother mumbo-jumbo. Fact is, I can sometimes be hard to handle when things don't go my way."

"I've noticed."

"I'm working on it. Forgive me?"

Hey, if he had the guts to admit when he was wrong, she had the grace to accept. "Water under the bridge."

They were traveling deeper and deeper into endless cornfields and they hadn't passed one single vehicle in the past fifteen minutes they'd been on the one-lane road. The sun was slipping toward the horizon. She suppressed the urge to turn around and go back the way they'd come. Only road construction waited for them back there. This was her bluff to snap Boone out of his grumpiness and she was stuck with it.

Hell, she wished she could turn the car over to him. Give the man the control he longed for. Sit back, relax and not have to worry about the trailer she was hauling behind her. But that was out of the question.

"How's the knee?" she asked.

"You don't have to keep asking about it. You're not my mother or my nursemaid."

"Don't get all defensive. I'm asking because I feel guilty for bouncing you all over the interstate."

"I'll live." He shifted in his seat.

She sneaked another quick glance at him. He looked amused and that surprised her. "What is it?"

"You should have seen the expression on your face when you left that highway." He chuckled. "All iron will and sheer determination, plowing over that median come hell or high water."

What do you know? She'd made him laugh. It hadn't been her intention, but she'd managed to make him laugh. Pleased with herself, Tara returned his grin.

"You've got spunk, Duvall. I like that about you."

"Wow. Another compliment. I'm stunned." She was teasing, but her heart gave a little hop.

"I've got a few more," he mumbled.

"How lucky can a girl get? What else do you like about me?"

"Your smart mouth. That's another thing."

"You like my smart mouth?"

"Oh, yeah." His gaze was fixed on her lips.

Her gaze was fixed on his eyes fixed on her lips. She wasn't watching where she was going, didn't see the board lying in the middle of the road, but she heard it.

Crunch, crunch, crunch.

Felt a jolt.

Followed by a rapid-fire popping sound. Once. Twice. Three times.

The car lurched, swerved. Startled, it took a moment for Tara to figure out what had happened.

Blowout.

Fudge crackers! She'd had a blowout.

Boone swore under his breath and he was already unbuckling his seatbelt.

Tara pulled over as far as she could on a one-lane dirt road with cornfields on either side. Simultaneously, she and Boone opened their car doors, but she was out before he was. He had the metal knee brace to contend with.

She walked to the rear of the car. Not one blown-out tire. Not two. But three flats. Both back tires of the Honda and one of the tires on the U-Haul were swiftly going flat. Hands on her hips, she went to investigate the heavy board lying behind the trailer and discovered a heavy two-by-four studded with nails.

Boone swore. He'd come around the opposite side of the trailer looking completely disgruntled. "Is the whole damned world against me?"

Tara shrugged.

He held up a finger. "Don't say it. Don't tell me Jupiter is in retrograde or—"

"Mercury," she said. "It's Mercury."

"I don't give a damn if it's Pluto. The planets did not cause this."

"Then what did?"

"A board with nails in it."

"That's small-picture thinking."

"What?" He shoved angry fingers through his hair, managing to appear both disgruntled and devastatingly sexy.

"On the surface, it appears that a board with nails caused our misfortune, but how did that board get here? On this particular one-lane road, just when we happened along? I mean, what are the odds?" She argued. "Bigger forces are afoot."

"You really believe in this zodiac stuff?"

"I do."

"What the hell does *retrograde* even mean?"

"Moving backward."

"So Mercury is moving backward?"

"Exactly."

"I fail to see how that can affect us."

"The moon affects the tides, right?"

"That's different."

"How so?"

"It's because the Earth and the moon are attracted to each other like magnets."

"If that's possible, why not Mercury? When Mercury is in retrograde, it can force fate upon us, usually in regard to something in the past that we need to resolve. Like your relationship with your sister."

"Let me get this straight. We have three flat tires because I have unresolved issues with my sister?"

Tara shrugged. "In a nutshell."

"Whacked." Boone shook his head, pulled his cell phone from his pocket. "The lemonade lady is whacked."

"Your cell's not going to work."

He glowered. "And why not?"

"One, because we're in the middle of nowhere and I haven't seen a cell phone tower in a long while. Two, Mercury is in retrograde and it affects travel plans and communications."

"You'll forgive me if I don't take your word for it."

She swept an expansive hand at him. "Be my guest."

Boone punched in a number, put the phone to his ear. A few fleeting seconds passed. He swore under his breath. Checked for bars. "Zero," he spat.

Tara pressed her lips together to keep from saying "I told you so."

He turned away from her. Limped out of her line of sight behind the U-Haul.

"Where are you going?" she asked.

"Detour," he called out.

Puzzled, she frowned, and then realized he was probably going to relieve himself, but didn't want to tell her that. The man had a skewed sense of pride. "Everybody needs a bathroom," she hollered after him. "It's okay to say the word."

A long moment passed. She leaned against the side of

the U-Haul, crossed her arms over her chest and stared west out over the cornfield at the setting sun.

Reality sank in.

It was going to be dark before long. They only had one spare tire, and even if they'd only had one flat, Boone was in no shape to change a tire. There was no cell phone reception and it was a very long walk back to the freeway. Not a trek Boone could make. They were stuck here until someone came along. No telling how long that might be.

The sun slipped a little lower. The air smelled loamy. Somewhere in the distance, a cow mooed. Tara drew a circle in the sand with the toe of her sandal, clutched her arms behind her back and swayed, waited.

Boone sure was taking his time. Honestly, no one needed that much time to do what he was doing. Tara nibbled her bottom lip, edged toward the cornrow. "Boone?"

He didn't answer.

The cornstalks threw eerie shadows across the road. She rounded the other side of the U-Haul, but he was nowhere in sight. Where had he gone?

"Boone? You there?"

Nothing. It was as if he'd simply vanished.

She thought of all the horror movies she'd seen. In horror movies, bad things always happened in cornfields.

"Boone?" she called again, surprised to hear her voice come out shaky. She wasn't a scaredy-cat by nature, but what if something had happened to him? He could have fallen in a gopher hole. He could be out there in the field, alone in the gathering dark, his knee wrenched, in terrible pain.

Throwing caution to the wind, she plowed through

the field. Cornstalks slapped against her shoulders. The setting sun blinded her. Panic built a dam in her chest. Why wasn't he answering?

"Boone!"

"What is it, Tara?" His deep voice sliced through the shivery cool twilight.

She spun around. Spied him standing behind her. Relief spilled into her bloodstream. "I thought…" She paused to catch her breath. "I thought you got lost. You're awfully stealthy for a big guy."

"Military training."

"Where'd you go?"

"I was looking for a place to set up camp."

"Set up camp?"

"Clearly we're not going anywhere anytime soon. It's best to make camp while we still have daylight left."

"Okay," she agreed. He was much calmer than she expected. She thought he'd bust another gasket over this current snafu like he had over the traffic snarl.

"Let's get some supplies." He turned to head back to the U-Haul.

Forty minutes later, they had set up camp on fallow ground just beyond the cornfield. Boone used blankets and curtain rods gleaned from the trailer. Tara had to do much of the work requiring physical dexterity because he had trouble navigating the uneven terrain of the field. Boone was the tent's architect. She was the builder.

He made a fire using a piece of flint and a folding knife fished from his pocket. He used the same knife to open a can of stew from the pantry items she'd packed for her move. If she had to get stranded, a quick-thinking soldier was the one to get stranded with. Boone was actually kind of fun when he had a mission. She even caught him whistling under his breath as he stirred the stew.

"Interesting," she said.

"What is?" He glanced up, and the last rays of sunlight caught his cheeks, bathing him in a red-orange glow that accentuated his rugged masculinity.

"You're not freaking out about this delay?"

"Maybe you're rubbing off on me," he said lightly. "Besides, it's my fault that we're here. If I hadn't been complaining about the construction log jam, you wouldn't have taken off down this side road to nowhere."

"True," she said, admiring his ability to admit his mistake. "But I'm just as much at fault. I let you get to me. I should have kept my cool."

"I guess we both overreacted, huh?"

"Stress can make anyone cranky. Too bad we're on a time crunch."

"I did the math. Worse case scenario, even with taking a day out of our travel to deal with this situation, I should be able to make it to Key West by early Saturday morning. The wedding isn't until the evening. That's enough time to set Jackie straight and put a stop to the whole thing."

She wondered how his sister was going to react to Boone swooping in and trying to stop her wedding. She started to say something to him, but it wasn't any of her business, so she just clamped her mouth shut. The stew smelled good and she realized they hadn't had anything to eat since they'd left the truck stop that morning.

Boone positioned a blanket on the ground near the fire and they sat side by side while he stirred the pot of food. He had his right leg stretched out in front of him and he'd taken off the heavy metal brace. Tara had her knees drawn up to her chest and she studied the dancing, orange-hot flames.

"This is nice," she said. "In spite of our circumstances. I like camping."

"Me, too. Or, at least I did before I went into the military."

"That changed you."

He shrugged. She could tell he didn't want to talk about it, so she didn't say anything else. Tara reached up to massage the kinks out of her neck. She was still sore from all that moving. If she was this knotted up, she could only imagine what shape Boone was in.

"Sore neck?" he asked.

"It's nothing."

"C'mere," he said. "I'll rub it for you."

"Will you?" she asked gratefully, before she understood what she was getting herself into.

He patted the blanket in front of him.

Tara edged over and sank down between his legs. The fire was in front of her, Boone behind. Talk about a rock and a hard place. Then his big hands touched her shoulders and began a gentle massage. She melted at the very same time she stiffened. Part of her wanting to relax into the moment, the other part on guard against the way his touch made her feel.

His fingers hit a tender spot.

"Ooh," she moaned.

"You've got a big knot there." He pushed in deeper, probing her sore muscle.

All the air left her body in one swift whoosh.

"Too hard?"

She shook her head. "Hurts so good."

"More?"

"Oh, yeah."

He increased the pressure. "How's that?"

"If it gets any better it's gonna be illegal."

His thumb made circular motions against her skin. "I can't believe how tense you are. You seem so loosey-goosey."

Yeah, except for when a sexy man was massaging her neck. "Appearances can be deceiving."

"You can say that again," he murmured.

"Appearances can be deceiving," she quipped, because his hands were moving lower, settling on her shoulders and she was getting some decidedly sweet sensations spreading over her.

"You're irrepressible."

"Like a wrinkled cotton shirt?"

"More like a bedspring."

A wild thrill fluttered against her ribcage, her skin tingling everywhere his fingers caressed her. "Coiled and ready for action?"

His laugh was so deep and rich, the flutter turned into an avalanche. The sensation was more than she could handle. She scooted away from him. "The stew is bubbling. I'm starving. Let's eat."

"Okay," he said.

Was it her imagination, or did he sound disappointed?

"I'll get the bowls." She returned with the mismatched bowls she'd dug from a box of kitchen supplies earlier.

He ladled stew into the bowls. "Spoons?"

She passed him an oversized spoon with an ornate handle, held a rounded soup spoon in her other hand.

"None of your dishes or silverware match," he said. "I noticed that when we were packing up."

"I buy them at garage sales. Cheap matters more to me than matchy-match."

He chuckled.

"What's funny?" Was he making fun of her frugality?

"Nothing."

"Stop laughing at me." She pretended to be miffed.

"I'm not laughing at you."

"No?"

"None of my dishes match either. I do the very same thing. I thought matching silverware mattered to women."

"Depends on the woman."

"No doubt."

She blew across the steaming spoonful of stew, but didn't meet his gaze. Her insides felt hot and shivery, like when you have a fever, and she had no idea why. "I would have thought that since you'd been married once, you'd have things that match."

"Naw. Shaina took the wedding gifts."

"She didn't leave you anything?"

"My freedom. Mismatched dishes. Small price to pay."

"Yeah," she said, as if she knew what she was talking about.

A long silence stretched between them. Tara felt the need to say something in order to keep from thinking too much. "You ever notice how food tastes better when it's cooked over an open flame?"

"You're just hungry."

"Seriously, there's something about the outdoors. The stars twinkling overhead. The smell of wood smoke…"

"We're burning cornhusks."

"The smell of cornhusk." Balancing her bowl of stew in one hand, Tara leaned forward on her knees to poke the fire with a stick. The flame hissed, flared high. She didn't know why she'd poked it, other than her rest- less need to move. It had nothing to do with the fact that Boone stirred feelings in her that no one else had ever stirred.

Liar, liar, pants on fire.

The heat was so intense that she jerked back, drop- ping both the stick and the bowl of stew. She gasped, and toppled backward onto Boone.

"Whoa." He grabbed her with an arm as strong as a steel band, momentarily holding her aloft in midair.

His wounded leg was between them. She twisted sideways, struggling not to fall on it. He was doing some fancy maneuvering himself to avoid the same thing. With his arm clutched tightly around her, he rolled onto his back, pulling her flush against him. Somehow, she ended up with legs dangling off to one side, skirt hem flipped up, her butt in the air and her pelvis pressed sideways against his lower abdomen.

She was so stunned, that for a second she just lay there, trying to figure out how she had gotten herself into this predicament.

Boone's body tensed beneath her weight and she felt something hard. Oh dear, was that…? Tara gulped.

He grew harder still. "Get off!" he hollered.

She scrambled up, spun around and sprinted toward the car, stumbling in the darkness, her cheeks burn- ing hotly.

Fudge on a cracker! She'd given Boone an erection.

DAMMIT!

He'd already apologized to her once and it had taken everything he could muster to admit he was wrong.

Asking for forgiveness felt like weakness and he was weak enough as it was with a bum leg.

But when her warm, tight body lay stretched across his he'd gotten aroused. It was a normal biological reaction. How could she blame him for something he had no control over? Was she insulted? Scared that he was going to take advantage of her? She'd run away from him. Clearly, he'd made her uncomfortable. Hell, he'd made himself uncomfortable. He didn't like facing the fact that flaky Tara Duvall turned him on.

Boone let loose with a stronger curse word. They were still a very long way from Key West. He had to do something to smooth things over. Apologize again, if needed. He winced and struggled to his feet. He didn't bother putting on his brace and he had to pick his way carefully over the uneven ground. In the light from the half-moon, he could make out her silhouette. She was leaning against the back of the U-Haul, her head bowed.

A spurt of alarm went through him. Was she that upset? Frig. Now he felt like a pervert.

"Tara," he said softly once he reached the trailer. A strange tugging pulled at his heart. "Are you okay?"

She made a noise, sort of a cross between a snort and a chortle, but she could have been crying. Really? Crying? She might be a lot of things—impulsive, nosy, a chatterbox, but he'd never thought of her as someone who got upset easily. Or someone who would be shocked over an impromptu reaction.

He limped closer. He could smell her natural fragrance mingling with the scent of the night. "Tara?"

Her shoulders shook helplessly.

Yep, she was crying. He hated it when women cried. Tears made him feel so useless. "Hey," he said simply. "Hey there. No need to snivel."

He touched her upper arm.

She turned into him. He wrapped his arms around her. "There, there, I didn't mean to yell at you. I didn't mean to get…aroused."

All at once he realized she wasn't crying, but laughing. She was laughing at him!

Irritated, he put her away from him. "Ha, ha, very funny."

"What? You thought I was crying because of how you spoke to me?" She lowered her eyelids, sent him a sultry look. "Or that I was shocked into sobs over your…" Her sly gaze slipped below his belt. "Um, impressive package?"

He flushed hot all over. "I didn't think *that*."

Her lip curled into an impish grin. "I did."

The woman was toying with him and enjoying getting a rise out of him. Literally. "You're hopeless."

"And you're uptight. Relax, Boone. The world isn't going to come to an end if you have a good laugh at yourself." She winked.

No matter how much he wanted to, he couldn't stay mad at her for long. For one thing, she was just so damned bewitching with that cocky little grin and rocking hot body. His hand itched to draw her close again, to run his fingers through her hair, tilt her head back and plant rough kisses along that long, slender neck. The caveman in him wanted to do much more than that. A dozen erotic images passed through his head.

The woman was a knockout. Slender, but not skinny. Long-legged. Breasts that were the stuff of dreams. Her blond hair was tousled, falling over her shoulders in a sexy tangle. She had skin the color of a ripe peach— honey-hued and golden—eyes the color of the Montana sky, full lips, a playful chin, sassy cheekbones. The way she spoke was light and airy, as if she lived in a bouncy-house castle made of clouds.

Her frisky pink tongue flicked out to skim nervously over her femme fatale lips.

Friggin' hell, he was in trouble here. His heart punched against his chest and a dull roar filled his ears.

His arms wrapped around her even as his mind yelled, *No, no, don't do it.*

Tara didn't resist, not the least little bit, as he pulled her flush against his chest until he could feel the rhythm of her throbbing heartbeat matching his own.

Her eyes widened, but she didn't seem at all scared or unnerved by his proprietary action.

What was he doing? It was dumb. It was a mistake. He knew it, but the feel of her in his arms, soft and pliant, was his undoing. Confusion settled inside him, but rising up to take its place was a dark, dangerous heat and the stunning realization of just how much he wanted her.

His gaze fixed on her mouth.

Her trembling lips parted.

He was quickly losing what was left of his self-control.

His face was inches from hers. He peered into her eyes, lost as a dingy in a squall. A taut, jolting look passed from him to her and back again. He realized for the first time that she had her hands around his biceps and was holding on tightly. To keep him from coming any closer? Or to encourage it?

The night breeze blew coolly against his heated skin and for a long while, they just stood there, frozen in time. The make-or-break moment. Would he be strong enough to stop this and walk away before he did something he would regret?

He could feel her warm breath against his chin, hear the rapid rising and falling of her chest. He was aware of everything about her. She was so sexy. He'd been resisting her allure for weeks, hell, months even. Trying to convince himself that hooking up with her would be a bad thing.

His body didn't care about reasons or excuses. It was too late for either. His primal brain was issuing a message he was helpless to resist or deny.

His arms tightened around her.

She went up on tiptoes and leaned into him.

Turn back. Turn back. It's still not too late. Just let her go. Move away.

But damn his hide, he did not let her go. He did not turn away. He did not walk off. Instead, Boone did what he'd been struggling hard not to do for the past two days.

He kissed her.

6

TARA BIT HIM.

Not hard, just a simple back-off-buster pinch of her teeth against the firm flesh of his bottom lip. It was a simple warning—as much for herself as for him—nothing more.

But instead of being warned off, a low laugh rolled from his throat, deep and masculine and delighted.

A flicker of panic ran through her. Not because she was scared or offended, but because the secret little fantasy she'd been indulging about her across-the-street neighbor was coming true.

He speared his good knee between her legs, pressed it against the U-Haul, effectively pinning her in place. She tried to rationalize that he was doing the maneuver to stabilize his weak leg, but still, she couldn't help feeling captured by him. She couldn't move with her legs on either side of his thigh. His hand held the back of her head, his fingers threaded through her hair. She couldn't have run away if she'd wanted to do so.

It turned her on in ways she'd never dreamed possible. Instantly, her body was wanting and ready.

Boone stared into her eyes. Stared into *her*. No nonsense. Manly. Tough. Take-no-prisoners.

Instantly, they both reacted, attacking each other's mouths like starving people let loose on an all-you-can-eat buffet, nothing subtle or timid about the approach. They kissed with gusto and verve.

Tara found herself clinging to him, pushing against him, getting as close as she could get without being joined to him. Pure sensation overpowered her. Hard, driving desire overwhelmed her. Every rational thought Tara possessed flew right out of her head. Bowled over by his raw animal magnetism, by the fiery tingling of her nerve endings and the intensity of his body heat, she wanted nothing more than to sink down on the hard-packed roadbed, make love to him and damn the consequences.

He was experiencing the same thing she was. She could feel it in his body, in his hot, fierce kisses.

Until this road trip, she'd thought her feelings for Boone were one-sided. She liked him, but he wasn't crazy about her. But now, the desperately hungry way he explored her mouth told her that he was just as lost as she. Marooned. They were marooned together on this tidal wave of stark, relentless need.

His tongue slid against hers, demanding and yet at the same time strangely gentle. She could feel the pressure of his swollen sex pressing against her belly as he leaned into her, the hard metal of the trailer cool against her back.

He nuzzled her neck at the same time his hands coasted down her body. His palms found her breasts. Her nipples peaked and his thumbs strummed over them, stirring the treacherous feelings churning inside her.

Desperate, wondrous yearning unfurled in the pit of her stomach, spiraling low and heavy, making her body quiver and her knees weaken. If his legs were as unsteady as hers, she had no idea how he remained standing. If he wasn't holding her up, she'd collapse. How was it that he was strong and stable in light of his injury?

The next thing she knew, his hand had slipped up under the hem of her dress, slid up her thigh. His warm, nimble lips still had control of her mouth as his bold hand caressed her heated skin.

His kisses alternated between bold and tender, sweet and salty. Kissing him was like eating a gourmet meal at a five-star restaurant. With the tip of his tongue, he explored—outlining the contours of her mouth, touching the sensitive area right below her ear that made her shiver uncontrollably.

It felt so good. This runaway lust was tempting and exquisitely dangerous, but she knew she had to stop it and stop it now, before she made a foolish mistake. She opened her mouth to tell him just that, but then he cupped her face between his palms and coaxed her tongue to come out and duel with his.

And for another long, blissful moment she was lost again.

A mournful howl echoed over the cornfields, followed by yipping noises that raised the hairs on Tara's arms.

Coyotes.

Reality shattered the moment. Common sense returned. They weren't near a bed. Boone had a bum leg. She was moving to Miami. He lived in Bozeman.

There was no way this could ever mean anything other than sex.

What's wrong with just sex?

Nothing. Nothing at all. Except...

Tara feared that one time with Boone would never, ever be enough. Better never to eat the tempting cheesecake than take a small bite that led to gobbling the entire thing. With him, it was all or nothing.

He must have come to the same conclusion, because they broke apart simultaneously, Boone swearing softly under his breath, Tara inhaling sharply. He almost lost his balance as he stepped away from her, but he managed to right himself without toppling over. Legs trembling, she wasn't in much better shape. She stood there with her back pressed against the door, afraid to move in case she did fall and nervous as hell about the feeling blooming inside her.

His eyes hooked on her face, his expression impassive. She had no idea what he was thinking or feeling. She had an urge to pull her shirt up over her face to hide from him. She was afraid of what he might see in her eyes.

She drew air into her lungs as deeply as she could against the tight band of emotion constricting her chest. He'd knocked her off kilter, both emotionally and physically, doing things to her with his wicked tongue that left her senseless. She'd kissed other guys before, but no kiss had ever made her feel like this.

"This..." She paused, exhaled.

"I know."

"It's—"

"No need to explain."

"I don't want you to—"

"Shh." He placed an index finger over her lips. "It's okay."

But it wasn't okay! "Boone, I want you, I want this but—"

"No," he said brusquely. Then, without another word, Boone turned and limped back toward their camp.

AN HOUR LATER, Boone lay under the stars, the back of his head resting in his upturned palms, his fingers interlaced, elbows extended. His knee ached, but he barely noticed because another body part ached even more.

From the makeshift tent beside him, he could hear Tara's soft, feminine snores. He smiled up at the sky. If he told her she snored, he knew she'd deny it six ways to Sunday.

He thought about the rough, demanding way he'd kissed her, driven by pure primal instinct. It scared him how easily he'd lost control. The mysterious, beguiling power Tara held over him bamboozled Boone. Why Tara?

What was it about her that so enthralled him? She was gorgeous, granted, but the attraction was more than that. Whenever Tara looked at him in that perky way of hers, he felt completely naked. As if she could see right through his defenses, understood him and liked him anyway. This was why he'd avoided her for so long. Deep down, he'd known she had the power to crack his foundation, and Boone was nothing if not dug in.

And then there was that kiss they'd shared.

Well, he didn't want to think about it, didn't want to label their relationship or read anything into the kiss. But he could still taste her salty-sweet flavor and he wanted more. So much more. That's what he'd been trying so hard to avoid—this disturbing fever-pitch level of intense longing.

Absent-mindedly, he licked his lips. He'd married Shaina and she'd never kissed him the way Tara did, full of reckless, determined intent. Once upon a time, he'd been infatuated with this ex-wife, but she'd never dominated his thoughts the way Tara did. A whole lot less passion than he felt for Tara had led him to a Vegas wedding chapel. That was the problem. He had no real internal barometer when it came to women.

Tonight had shown him just how explosive he and Tara were together. They had been fully into each other and the more they'd tasted, the more they wanted. He thought of how the cheek of her sweet ass had felt cupped in his palm, only the flimsy material of her underwear between his hand and her bare skin, and Boone groaned out loud.

How far would they have taken it if the sound of coyotes hadn't pulled them apart? Would he have had the presence of mind to stop on his own? He liked to think so, but Tara had a way of turning him inside out and upside down. Whenever he was around her, he found himself wanting…well, what did he want from her?

Sex, obviously, but it was more than that. She had qualities that, even though he might moan about them, secretly appealed to Boone. He liked her quirkiness and how she kept him off guard. For instance, he didn't know any other woman who would have taken that U-Haul off-road. Impulsive yes, but brave. Plus, she was a problem solver. Granted, things had not turned out the way she'd planned, but he had to admire a woman who took action.

He closed his eyes, struggled to sleep. He kept smelling her scent, seeing her smile, tasting her lips, hearing her breathing and feeling her supple skin beneath his fingertips. He wished…hell…he wasn't even going to try to articulate what he wished.

Dumb.

This was dumb and useless. There was no point longing for things that weren't good for him. The military had taught him to control his urges, to face temptation head-on and plow his way through things. But the army never bargained on a force of nature like Tara Duvall. That seductive sway of hers could coax a saint into sinning.

The night breeze blew over him. Even though it was early July, it was still cool in the dampness of the fallow field. He sat up and poked at the fire, stirring the embers for warmth.

Remember why you're here. You're on the road to stop your sister from marrying the wrong man.

That did the trick. Thinking about Jackie got his mind off Tara. At least for a few minutes, but the trouble was that thinking about Jackie made him realize that he might not get to Key West in time. Not with this detour. What if no one came along in the morning?

To keep from fretting, he did mental math. Tomorrow was Thursday. They were sixteen hundred miles from Miami. If they drove an average of sixty miles per hour then it would take about twenty-six hours. He had to factor in at least four stops. If by some miracle someone came by, they got the car repaired and were back on the road by noon tomorrow, he could reasonably expect to get to Key West by late Friday night or early Saturday morning. Still plenty of time to stop Jackie's late-afternoon wedding. But that was assuming everything went well.

Boone never assumed anything, and he always prepared for the worst, but what he'd never factored in was getting in the path of Hurricane Tara.

THE SOUND OF a tractor woke Tara at dawn.

She came out of the tent blinking, yawning and stretching. Boone was sitting on the blanket, strapping the metal brace to his leg. He stopped in midmotion, his gaze fixed on her.

She realized then that the oversized T-shirt she slept in had risen up along with her stretch, revealing the edge of her pink panties. Struggling against the heat that flooded her cheeks, she ducked her head and immediately lowered her arms.

"Pink?" One quizzical eyebrow arched on his forehead.

Tara pretended she hadn't heard him. Somehow, the knowledge that Boone had seen her underwear bothered her more than the kiss they'd shared the night before. There was something just too intimate about it. Quickly, she found her blue jeans and tugged them on, almost tripping herself in her haste.

The sound of the tractor grew louder.

"Someone's coming," she said.

"I was trying to get my brace on and get out into the road to wave them down," Boone explained.

"I'll do it," Tara offered.

He gave a fake cough, glanced at her chest.

She straightened, glanced down and saw that her erect nipples were poking through the thin cotton material of her T-shirt. Good grief!

Boone's mouth pulled up in a smirk, even though she could see him fighting against it. "You might want to put on a bra."

Sexual tension vibrated between them and her breath

slipped rapidly between her teeth as she imagined exactly what he must have been thinking. She nibbled a thumbnail, glanced around on the pretense of finding her bra, but honestly, she was just trying to look anywhere but into his eyes.

Then she remembered she'd left it inside the tent. She crawled back inside, found her bra, wrestled it on and then stepped back outside.

In the meantime, Boone had made it to his feet. He wore the same cargo shorts he'd had on the day before, and he had his hands clasped behind his back. His gaze grazed over her, moving from the top of her tousled hair, to the slope of her breasts (now safely harnessed), to the thighs of her snug-fitting jeans on down to her bare feet.

"Have you seen my flip-flops?" she asked, feeling flustered, her pulse pounding erratically.

He pulled them out from behind his back. "You're a bit scattered. I found them in the field last night and thought about hiding them from you just to teach you to pay attention."

"So, why did you take pity on me?"

"I realized it's not my place to change you. And, you need them to flag down the tractor. You can get out there before I can."

"It kills you, doesn't it?" she asked, and from the glint in his eyes she knew it was true.

"I hate being helpless," he said. "*H-A-T-E,* hate it."

She leaned forward to put on her flip-flops, teetering on one foot and then the other. Boone put out a hand to steady her. An immediate heat flamed through Tara. His touch had always revved her up, but after last night, she seemed extra sensitive toward him.

"Are you okay?" he asked hoarsely.

"Sure, fine, terrific, great," she chattered. "Why wouldn't I be okay?"

"You've got goose bumps." Gently, he moved his hands up and down her forearms as if to warm her.

It only made the goose bumps worse and kicked her heart rate into a gallop. For a long, agonizing second, she couldn't speak. All she could do was absorb the warmth of his skin.

The sound of the tractor chugging into an idle snapped her from the spell Boone had woven over her. "Tractor's here," she said, yanking her hand away to wave at the green vehicle that had come to a stop behind the U-Haul.

Then, she turned and raced toward the farmer, feeling both unsettled and relieved.

THE FARMER'S NAME was Paul Brown and it was his field they'd spent the night in. Paul graciously volunteered to give them a ride to Fairville, the closest town. Paul went back to his house and returned with a pickup truck. Hopefully, they could find a place to shower and change their clothes in town. Boone took his knapsack from the Honda and Tara retrieved her overnight bag.

For the entire twenty-minute trip, Boone kept glancing at his watch. Tara knew he was nervous about making it to Key West, but they had plenty of time. It was only Thursday morning and his sister's wedding wasn't until late Saturday afternoon. Boone was a fretter. She could reassure him all day long and he would still worry, so she didn't even bother.

She sat in the cab of the pickup, sandwiched between Paul and Boone. The truck smelled like hay, motor oil and Nebraska loam. Reaching over, she laid a hand on Boone's good knee, just to let him know that she understood, but the second her fingers settled on his bare skin, she knew that touching him had been a mistake.

His muscles were so firm and masculine. With every pump of blood that pushed through her veins she was aware of everything about him—the sound of his breathing, the tension in his body, the smell of his scent, unique and utterly male. Her own body tightened and it felt as if—

Knock it off!

She slipped her hand off his knee, shifted her attention to Paul and started bombarding him with questions about farming, anything to get her mind off Boone.

Paul, she learned, had been born and raised in Fairville and he thought Nebraska was heaven on earth. His wife's name was Peggy and they had three kids, all of whom were grown and living elsewhere. That saddened him quite a bit.

"Young people today." Paul shook his head. "You're always in such a blasted hurry. Always on your computers and whatever else is the new-fangled thing of the day. Do they ever pick up the phone and just make a call?"

"But you know," Tara pointed out, "because of social media, people are actually more connected. My mom texts me every day."

"It's not the same as hearing their voices," Paul complained. "Hell, for all I know someone stole their phones and is sending those text messages."

"Paul's got a point," Boone pointed out. "A lot has been lost in our technological world."

"And that cyber-bullying," Paul put in. "It's ten times worse than when I was kid. Back in those days, if you wanted to stand up to a bully, you took boxing lessons.

Nowadays, those poor kids have no recourse. Some even end up taking their lives over it. Such a damn shame."

"Look at all the advantages technology provides," Tara said. "We can go online and pay our bills—"

"Leaving us wide open to identity theft."

"We can send messages instantly. No need to wait for letters."

"It's killing the post office." Paul readjusted his green John Deere cap on his head.

"But saving trees."

Paul laughed and glanced over at Boone. "Your wife's a feisty one. She could argue the hind leg off a donkey. I bet you never win a disagreement with her."

"We're not married," Boone rushed to say.

Paul looked surprised. "Really? You two look so good together, I just assumed."

"She's just giving me a ride to Miami."

Wow, Boone couldn't wait to set Paul straight, as if being married to her was such a terrible notion. Tara felt as if she'd swallowed a walnut whole and it had gotten stuck in her throat.

Paul's smile turned sly. "Well, you never know. Road trips have a way of breeding romance. That's how I fell in love with Peggy. Senior class trip to Padre Island. Before that, we couldn't stand each other. Her family had money and she was a cheerleader and I thought she was stuck-up. She thought I was a know-it-all, but by the time we got to the Gulf of Mexico we were madly in love. Been happily married thirty-seven years and countin'."

"That's such a sweet story," Tara said.

"You never know when love is gonna sneak up on you," Paul waxed philosophical. "Just remember, there's a reason they say opposites attract. If you're both the same, where's the spark? Where's the sizzle? Where's the mystery?"

"But you have to have some common ground in order to stay married for so long. I bet you and Peggy have more in common than you think," Tara argued.

"You're right there. We both value family, tradition and the American farm."

"See, there. Not so opposite after all."

"You're a pistol, Tara. Smart and pretty." Paul leaned forward, to get a better look at Boone. "You're dumber than you look, son, if you let this one get away. She's a treasure."

Tara's cheeks heated and she cast a quick glance over at Boone to see how he was taking Paul's advice. His face was impassive.

"She is special," Boone said.

Hmm. Special. What did that mean? The word had so many connotations. Not all of them good.

7

PAUL DROPPED THEM off at a local garage and they spoke to a mechanic, who agreed to go out to Paul's farm and tow Tara's Honda and the U-Haul trailer back to his shop to replace the tires.

"You folks might as well relax," said the mechanic, who had the name *Ross* embroidered across the front pocket of his work shirt. He had a Tweety Bird tattoo on his left forearm, wore his hair slicked back in a greasy ducktail like a 1950s rebel and had a toothpick tucked into the corner of his mouth. "It's gunna be a few hours. I'm here by myself until nine."

Boone grunted, looked displeased.

Tara gave Ross a friendly smile. "Is there a place nearby where we might clean up? We spent the night in Paul Brown's field and I really need a shower."

Ross got a lascivious grin on his face, as if he were imagining Tara in the shower, and stared pointedly at her breasts. She pretended she didn't see the look.

Boone saw it. He growled, clenched his fists at his sides. She could tell he was about to say something. In order to stop him from upsetting Ross—they had to stay on the mechanic's good side if they wanted her tires repaired in a timely manner—she linked her arm through Boone's, rested her head against his shoulder and mentally sent the message *shut up.* If they came across as a couple, Ross was much less likely to ogle her.

Boone took the hint. Or maybe he was just unnerved by the fact she'd taken his arm.

She tried not to notice how powerful his biceps were or how the feel of his muscles stoked her engines. Canting her head, she studied Ross expectantly. "Any motels within walking distance?"

"No," Ross said. "But there's a bed-and-breakfast at the end of the block. Tell Mrs. Hubbard I sent you over and she'll give you a discount rate since you just need a shower and a place to crash until your car is ready."

"Thank you." Tara rewarded him with a cheery smile.

Ross grinned back. "I'll have your car ready by noon."

"I do so appreciate it. C'mon, honey," she said to Boone, and with her arm still linked through his, guided him out the door.

"'Honey'?" Boone said, amusement in his voice after they'd stepped into the early morning sunlight.

"A reminder. You can catch more flies with honey than you can with vinegar."

"Sometimes you make no sense to me at all," he admitted.

"Just putting on a show for our friend back there." Immediately, she slipped her arm from his so she could breathe a little easier. Standing so near him, touching him so intimately, knocked her off kilter. "Thank you for not going off on him like you did on the movers."

"I'm learning," he said. "Although it's a challenge reining in my inner caveman around you. Every guy wants you."

"Not every guy."

"Damn near. You're too gorgeous for your own good."

Flattered, she briefly pressed a palm to her mouth. "It's not your place to defend me."

"I know," he said and sounded so regretful that Tara sent him a sharp look. "I have no claims on you."

"Nor do you want them," she pointed out.

"Nor do I want them," he echoed half-heartedly.

A prickle of something she couldn't name poked at her. *Don't read anything into it. Even if he does like you, what does it matter? You're going to be living at opposite ends of the country.*

"There's the B&B," she pointed out, happy to have something else to discuss.

The Rose Garden Resort was a stately Victorian home, painted blue with yellow gingerbread trim. Numerous rosebushes bloomed in profusion along a white picket fence. A red paving-stone walkway led to the front door. Boone followed her up the path. She could feel him behind her.

This is a man who will always have your back.

Too bad it didn't matter. He wasn't her man. Never would be. But she found herself hoping that one day she'd have a partner like Boone, someone who'd have her back, no matter what.

Strange. She'd never had an impulse or wish like this before. She was an independent, free spirit. She didn't need anyone sheltering her.

Didn't need it, no, but suddenly, she *wanted* it.

You're worn out from packing, moving and driv-

*ing. You're dirty and hungry. That's all it is. You're ex-
hausted and the idea of having someone take care of
you sounds good. What you're feeling is nothing more
than that.*

They stepped up onto the wide, welcoming, wrap-
around veranda. On the front porch was a sign that in-
structed them to come on in. Tara opened the screen
door. The sound of Mozart and the scent of lavender
greeted them. To the left was a sweeping staircase with
an ornate cherry-wood banister. To the right was a small
reception desk constructed from the same cherry wood.

A smiling older woman, who looked exactly like a
Mrs. Hubbard, stood behind the desk. She wore a ging-
ham apron and oversized tortoiseshell spectacles. She
was dusting a shelf of knickknacks, and oddly enough,
given that Mozart was on the sound system, she sang
an off-key rendition of B.B. King's "When Love Comes
to Town."

"Good morning!" she greeted them.

"Ross from the garage sent us," Tara said. "We're just
passing through and need a place to freshen up while
we're having our car worked on."

"So you'll just be needing the room for a few hours?"

"That's right."

Mrs. Hubbard shifted her gaze to Boone. "Just one
room?"

"Two," Boone said, reaching for his wallet.

"One will do," Tara said. "No sense paying extra
when we can take turns showering." She didn't realize how suggestive that sounded until it was out of her
mouth. "I mean, not that we were both going to shower
at the same time. We don't shower together. We…" Ack!
She was just making things worse. Tara clamped her
mouth shut.

Behind her, Boone let out a soft chuckle. "One room. Consecutive showering."

Mrs. Hubbard arched a speculative eyebrow. "Do you want to include breakfast?"

"Yes," Boone said. "Charge us for two breakfasts."

Her eyes twinkled behind her big glasses. "Consecutive?"

"Concurrent."

"Very good. Breakfast is in the dining room, just through that door." The woman pointed.

"Food or shower first?" Boone asked Tara as they walked away from the reception desk.

"Food," she said, not just because her stomach was growling, but also because she just wasn't ready to be alone with Boone in a bedroom.

The dining room was empty, save for a man in a business suit reading *The Wall Street Journal* by the window. The food was served buffet style from chafing dishes. The smell of bacon had Tara's mouth watering. They filled their plates and sat down across from each other at a small table. Tara spread a napkin over her lap. Boone paused to look at his watch again.

"Staring at your watch isn't going to make time go faster," she observed.

"Don't want it to go faster. Want it to slow down."

"What time is it?"

"Eight-thirty."

"Nothing we can do about it. Might as well relax and enjoy the day."

He canted his head at her. "How do you do it?"

"What?" She speared a forkful of fluffy scrambled eggs.

"The whole lemonade thing."

She shrugged. "I'd rather be happy than in turmoil."

He shook his head. "Wish I could do that."

"It's easy. Just look at the bright side."

"Which is?"

"You're still mobile."

"Barely."

"You're good-looking."

He snorted.

"What? You don't think you're good-looking?"

"Looks are inconsequential. They don't last."

"You're a millionaire."

"Thanks to my father."

"You're not balding."

He finally cracked a smile and ran a hand through his thick head of hair. "You got a point."

"See? There's always a bright side." The bright side for her was that she was having breakfast with the handsome man who would never have eaten breakfast with her back in Bozeman, but she didn't tell Boone that, of course.

"These blueberry pancakes are really good," he admitted.

"One way or another, bit by bit, I'll seduce you to the sunny side of life," Tara predicted.

Seduce.

Why had she said that word? It lay there between them like an unexploded hand grenade. Light shone in through the window, bathing Boone's face in sunshine. Stubble ringed his angular jaw, lending him a dangerous air. The sleeves of his shirt were rolled up, revealing the strong forearms thick with dark hair.

"I think you're deeper than that."

"What?"

"I think you choose to be happy because you're

scared what will happen if you let yourself experience negative feelings."

Alarm had her smiling doubly hard. How had he guessed that about her?

"You pump up the energy around you by laughing and joking and having a good time, but it's just a cover."

"It's not," she said, concerned that he'd seen through her most basic insecurity about herself and annoyed by the little flare of panic that ignited in her at his assessment. He'd cut close to the bone.

"You're afraid of painful feelings."

"Isn't everyone?"

He shook his head. "No. Pain is a part of life. You can't truly appreciate joy until you've suffered."

"Well then, you must be on the verge of becoming Mr. Freaking Sunshine because you've suffered a hell of a lot."

His smile was rueful. "I've made you mad."

"Me?" She screwed up her face in an expression of denial, shook her head, shrugged.

"See? You don't even want to feel that negative emotion."

"You're pushing your luck, Boone. I'm just a happy person."

"Yeah?"

"Yes."

"Okay, what was the first thing you did when you heard about your mother's breast cancer diagnosis?"

Tara squashed a blueberry with the back of her fork. "I went to play softball."

"I rest my case."

"What? It wasn't like I could change the diagnosis. What was I supposed to do? Wring my hands? Gnash my teeth? Shake my fist at the sky and curse God?"

"Most people would have done some version of that, but you go play softball."

A sick feeling settled in the pit of her stomach. "Does that make me a terrible daughter?"

"No, it makes you the kind of person who masks her pain by trying to lift her mood."

"What did you do?" she asked. "When you found out your dad had died?"

"I got my pistol, went to the junkyard my friend owned and shot the hell out of an old rusted-out car."

"Oh, yes, that's so much healthier than playing softball."

"I'm not saying the way you handle negative emotions is wrong, simply pointing it out because I'm not sure you're aware of it."

"Thanks, now I know. I enjoy having my flaws brought to my attention."

He reached across the table, touched her hand. "You need to know that it's okay to feel bad sometimes."

"You should know. You've made feeling bad a true art form."

He raised his palms. "You're right. I'm out of line. I shouldn't have said anything."

But he wasn't out of line. He'd hit the nail on the head, and Tara knew it. The character trait that had caused her the most trouble was the inability to take life seriously.

Boone was looking at her with such kind compassion that her gut wrenched. Here she'd been trying so hard to get him to cheer up when he'd actually seen benefit in his low mood. It was a foreign concept to her.

Opposites attract.

Tara quickly pushed back her plate. "I'm ready for a shower."

Send For
2 FREE BOOKS
Today!

I accept your offer!

Please send me two free
Harlequin® Blaze® novels and
two mystery gifts (gifts worth
about $10). I understand that
these books are completely
free—even the shipping and
handling will be paid—and I am
under no obligation to purchase
anything, ever, as explained on the
back of this card.

151/351 HDL FNN5

Please Print

FIRST NAME

LAST NAME

ADDRESS

APT.#   CITY

STATE/PROV.   ZIP/POSTAL CODE

Visit us online at
www.ReaderService.com

Offer limited to one per household and not applicable to series that subscriber is currently receiving.

Your Privacy—The Reader Service is committed to protecting your privacy. Our Privacy Policy is available online at www.ReaderService.com or upon request from the Reader Service. We make a portion of our mailing list available to reputable third parties that offer products we believe may interest you. If you prefer that we not exchange your name with third parties, or if you wish to clarify or modify your communication preferences, please visit us at www.ReaderService.com/consumerchoice or write to us at Reader Service Preference Service, P.O. Box 9062, Buffalo, NY 14269. Include your complete name and address.

A wry smile lifted one corner of Boone's mouth.

Hmm, that sounded suggestive, too. "Um, could I have the room key?"

He pulled the room key Mrs. Hubbard had given him from his shirt pocket, but made no move to come with her, thank heavens. Her chest felt oddly tight as she scurried from the dining room, up the creaky stairs and located room 201. Not that it was a challenge. There were only three bedrooms on the second floor.

She rushed in, dropping her overnight bag on the floor in her haste, barely even noticing that the room was decorated in rose floral wallpaper. She went straight to the bathroom, closing the door behind her. That's when she caught sight of her reflection in the oval mirror over the white porcelain sink.

Holy tornado. She looked like she'd been through a Kansas twister and Tara knew firsthand what that was like.

Her hair was a mess. No, *mess* was too kind. It was a tangled rat's nest. The mascara she hadn't removed last night before falling into the tent had smeared, making her look like Cleopatra on a drinking binge. Lovely.

After a sizzling-hot shower, she felt infinitely better and came out of the bathroom wrapped in a towel, her wet hair done up in a French braid.

Boone lay stretched out across the lone queen-sized bed, his hot gaze eating her up.

She startled and clutched the towel tighter around her. "What are you doing here?"

"You were the one who wanted one room. Consecutive showers, remember? I hope you left some hot water for me." He waved at the steam rolling out the bathroom door behind her.

"You were supposed to stay in the dining room until I finished."

"You never explained the rules," he said, his dark eyes searing her to the spot.

"How'd you get in?"

"You didn't lock the door behind you," he said, and then added, "I locked it."

The door was locked? They were locked in here together? Tara gulped, felt her stomach twitch. This was one of the negative emotions he'd been talking about.

Fear.

Not of him, but of herself and the impulse sprinting through her.

"Anyone could have followed you in here," he said in a calm, measured, but no-nonsense tone.

"So, that's it," she said. "You're trying to teach me a lesson. People can't be trusted. Duly noted. Now please get out while I get dressed."

"You're throwing me out of the room I paid for?" he drawled.

"Only until I get dressed." She was very self-conscious and acutely aware of how little there was between them. Her towel. His jeans.

"You can dress while I'm in the shower." He eased off the bed. His fingers curled around the strap of his knapsack and he came toward her.

Her pulse raced. Her heart thundered.

Get out of his way, you silly twit.

She stepped aside, held her breath as he passed within touching distance.

Just before he stepped into the bathroom, he reached behind her, and gently tweaked her braid. "Love the hair," he said and shut the door.

Lightning-quick, in case he popped unexpectedly

from the shower and caught her naked, she changed into a pair of white shorts and a red-and-white-striped V-neck T-shirt with three-quarter sleeves and exchanged her flip-flops for sneakers. She wore white "no show" socks with jaunty red pom-poms at the heels. She glanced at the clock. It was barely past nine. They had hours to kill before the car would be ready.

The shower came on.

Unbidden, instant images of Boone's naked body underneath the spray of water shot into her mind. She traced two fingers over her bottom lip, remembered the kiss they'd shared the night before. The kiss of the year? C'mon, it was more like the kiss of the decade. Decade? Right. Be honest.

It was the kiss of a lifetime.

She'd had the kiss of her lifetime. No sense trying to repeat it. Any further kissing was bound to be a letdown, nothing to do but seal that pristine kiss in her memory and move on.

Sure, and she had the willpower for that. Ha! If she stayed in this room alone with him, she would kiss him again, and if he kissed her like he kissed last night she wouldn't be able to stop. There was a reason she didn't eat potato chips. She couldn't stop with just one.

Boone was a potato chip.

She had to find something else to occupy their time. Determined, she bound downstairs to find Mrs. Hubbard watching *Good Morning America* on a tablet computer.

"Hi!" Tara greeted her breathlessly. "What do people do around here for fun?"

Mrs. Hubbard glanced up. "Usually guests come here from Lincoln or Omaha for a quiet romantic getaway."

She winked. "Most never leave their bedrooms except to come out for food."

"Isn't there anything to do around here?" she asked, desperate to fill the time until her car was ready. If she and Boone were caged up in the bedroom, she couldn't be held responsible for her actions. Being in close quarters with him was just too intoxicating. Cheap wine didn't go to her head as quickly as he did. Keeping her distance was the only way to play it safe and how did she keep her distance when she was stuck in a car or a room with the guy?

"There's Pine Lake. It's about three miles north of town."

"Anything within walking distance?"

"Hmm." Mrs. Hubbard stroked her chin. "On the weekends we have cooking and gardening classes, but this is Thursday."

"Golf course? Exercise class?" Tara was grasping at straws, knowing he couldn't do either of those things, but she and Boone both needed something to release the tension.

"Well…" The old woman paused.

"What, what?"

"There is the shooting range," Mrs. Hubbard suggested. "It's two blocks over."

"Perfect!" Tara said. This was exactly what she needed to keep Boone occupied.

8

WAS THERE ANYTHING sexier than a good-looking woman who knew how to handle herself? Until this minute, Boone had not realized exactly how erotic that scenario could be.

Tara stood at the firing line gripping the rented 9mm Smith & Wesson Sigma in both hands. A pair of protective safety glasses perched on her pert little nose. Her hair was still damp and pulled back in that fancy-looking braid that showed off her profile. White denim shorts hugged her shapely ass and he couldn't stop his gaze from tracking down her long, lean legs. Oh, those legs.

Instantly, his body tightened.

Boone wasn't even sure why he was here, except it beat sitting around Ross's greasy garage and watching him ogle Tara. Or hanging out at the B&B, getting lathered up over Tara prancing out of the bathroom in a towel.

The air smelled of gunpowder and gun oil. Down-range was a life-sized paper target of a human male.

Tara gazed coolly along the sight of her gun. Her biceps tensed, showing off nicely toned arms. With steady precision, she fired off three rounds. Boom. Boom. Boom. She absorbed the recoil of the gun without flinching. The echo rang around the concrete bunker as each shot struck the target in the torso.

Tara turned to grin at him.

"Not bad." Boone shrugged, trying to pretend that he wasn't duly impressed. Who knew she possessed such skills?

"Would it kill you to say 'well done'?"

"Might."

"You'd rather saw off your arm than pay someone a compliment, huh?"

"You did all right." Why couldn't he praise her?

"Okay? Oh, my, your generosity is making me dizzy." She set her gun on the firing bench and stepped back as was protocol at a firing range, demonstrating that she clearly knew the rules. She pressed the back of her hand to her forehead in a dramatic gesture. "I'm gonna swoon."

To Boone's alarm she tipped backward and for one split second he thought she really was fainting and then he realized she meant for him to catch her. Instinctively, he took a sideways step, arms wide.

She fell limply into his open embrace.

Boone stared down at her, his heart knocking crazily. How could she be so completely trusting? If he hadn't caught her, she would have busted her butt on the cement floor. She'd gone down easy as mashed potatoes, as if she'd been utterly certain he'd be there for her.

And he had been.

She gazed up at him, winked wickedly. "Nice catch."

He made a noise of irritation and set her on her feet.

"See how that works? You do something good, I compliment you."

Boone just growled.

"You don't fool me, Boone Toliver. Not one little bit. I know why you growl. You're scared to death someone's going to figure out what a softy you really are inside." She reached over and patted his flat belly.

Boone froze against the onslaught of sensation her touch stirred. Ah, man. He'd fought hard against it, but somehow she'd burrowed under his skin and had gotten to him.

She grinned and damn his hide, he couldn't stop himself from smiling back. Staying irritated with her was on par with kicking a puppy.

He thought he'd known his neighbor. He'd dismissed her as a beautiful, silly, overly friendly airhead. Boone saw that he'd done Tara a grave disservice. Sure, she was a gregarious chatterbox who could talk for hours about fashion and hairstyles, but she was so much more than that. She was warm and witty and insightful, and she sure knew how to handle a gun.

"Your turn," she said and handed him the weapon. "You deserve to let off some steam and I can't think of a better way to do that than blasting holes through a target and pretending it's everything that's bugging you."

Except that you're what's bugging me. The way you make me feel is dangerous as hell.

He was overstating. No. She was not dangerous. Not at all. Because after they reached Miami, he'd never see her again.

Why did that thought sadden him? He'd be happy to get her out of his hair once and for all. She was a pest. A cheery pest, granted, but a pest nonetheless. He wouldn't miss her. Not one bit.

"I wanna see what you've got. Show me you can do better." Her eyelids lowered seductively.

Her flirtatious tone issued a challenge not entirely related to shooting guns, and he knew it. There was nothing shy or retiring about Tara. He admired her openness at the same time he longed to run away from it. She made him feel transparent. As if she could see straight through all his defenses and there was no place for him to hide.

"Bring it on," he said.

She changed out the target, and Boone moved up to the firing line, careful with his stance, favoring his injured leg. He raised the gun. Bam. Bam. Bam. Three kill shots. Right through the heart.

"Wow," Tara exclaimed. "That was awesome."

He lowered the gun, shrugged.

"You're a crack marksman."

"I'm a soldier."

"Were."

"Huh?"

"You were a soldier."

"Yeah. Go ahead. Rub it in."

"I don't mean to make you feel badly about yourself. It's just that sometimes we all need a kick in the pants to help us get going again. Living in denial isn't a healthy place to hang out."

"And you got your degree in psychology from where?"

She stared at him for a second, a flicker of hurt moving across her face.

Damn it. He was such a jerk. He turned back to the target. Put two rounds clean through the target's forehead.

"That'll show 'em," she murmured under her breath.

Okay, so it might be a little obvious to take his frustrations out on the target, but it felt good. Already, the tension was draining from his shoulders. She'd been right to suggest this outlet.

"Want another turn?" he asked.

They shot a few more rounds, then returned the rental gun and left the shooting range. Tara walked slowly up the sidewalk beside him in concession to his limp. He hated that she had to adjust to his poky pace.

"Where'd you learn to shoot like that?" he asked.

"My dad and brothers are avid hunters. My father insisted we all learn how to shoot and he was rabid about gun safety."

"Have you ever been hunting?"

"Just skeet and targets. I'm too soft-hearted to kill animals."

Yeah, and here I am, a soldier. But not anymore. His career was gone. He'd loved the army. Loved the structured life. Without it, he felt adrift, purposeless. That was the root of his discontent. The loss of his identity.

But hanging out with Tara was starting to teach him there were other ways of being. She took each day as it came with good humor and a sense of adventure. She made him want to change. To let go of some of the restraint that had held him together for so long and just breathe.

Boone was so busy thinking about it that he didn't notice the fissure in the sidewalk. The toe of his shoe caught on the cracked cement. He stumbled, lurched.

Tara put out a hand, caught his elbow, and stabilized him. He regained his balance. Shame burned his face. Her chest was pressed against his arm as she held him steady.

Her nipples hardened beneath her shirt. Or was it just his wishful imagination?

"You okay?" Her breath warmed his ear.

Goose bumps spread down his neck in spite of the late-morning sun. He clenched his teeth. *Knock it off, Toliver. Just stop reacting to her.* Easy to say, much harder to will his body not to have a normal male response to a sexy woman.

Gently, he shook her off. "I'm fine."

"You don't look fine."

"I am."

"You look…" She paused, narrowed her eyes.

Boone kept walking.

Tara hurried to catch up. "You can run but you can't hide."

"Watch me," he called over his shoulder.

"I'm not letting you off the hook."

He had to slow down because his knee was throbbing.

"What are you so scared of Boone?"

You. No one had ever turned him upside down the way Tara did. "Not one damn thing."

"It's okay to be afraid."

No it wasn't. Not for him. Didn't she get that? He was the strong one. The protector. He wasn't supposed to get hurt. If he wasn't a soldier, then who the hell was he?

He stopped walking, turned to her on the quiet street of a small town he'd never been in before and would likely never be in again.

Tara stopped abruptly, mere inches from him. She titled her chin up and met his hard-edged stare without blinking. The way she looked at him made him feel… well, like the past was truly gone and all that mattered was the present. How did she do it? How did she live in the moment? He was envious of her skill and resented it at the same time.

"Boone," she said, reading his mind. "You can set your own course in life. Be whoever or whatever you want to be."

"I can't be a soldier."

"Not anymore, but you've already been there, done that. You're beyond that. It's time to move on."

"How?"

"By understanding that it's okay to be in transition. You don't have to have all the answers all the time."

"What if I can't change?"

"You can. You are already changing. Two weeks ago would you have possibly imagined you'd be on a car trip with me?"

"No."

"See there. You're on the road to change."

"Not willingly."

"Reluctantly or not, you went along for the ride. You did it. You're giving life a chance even if it feels like you're still mired in the mud. You'll get there."

"How can you be so sure?"

"Because every day is a journey. We're all a work in progress."

"Are *you* afraid?" he asked.

"All the time," she admitted. "But I don't let it stand in my way."

He didn't believe it. She was one of the bravest people he knew. "What are you afraid of?"

"You," she whispered. "This."

The next thing he knew, she reached up, captured his face between her palms and kissed him on the lips, light and quick like a butterfly landing on a flower. Then she

scurried, head down, into the mechanic shop, leaving
Boone staring after her in amazement.

IF SOMEONE HAD asked Tara why she'd kissed Boone,
she could have come up with only one answer that ad-
equately explained her impulse.

He looked like he needed it.

The minute her lips had touched his, she'd felt his
taut muscles soften. Heard his ragged intake of breath.
Then, for the span of two heartbeats, he'd done nothing
and she'd panicked. Right. He wasn't interested in kissing her. She'd made a gigantic fool of herself.

Why, oh why, had she kissed him? She should have
learned something from the previous night. Thankfully,
she'd had the sense to pull the plug and run away. Yet
she couldn't help wondering. Would he have kissed her
back if she hadn't?

She sneaked a glance over at Boone as he paid the
mechanic and she was surprised to see a pleasant expression on his face. Well, apparently she'd cheered him
up at least. That was good.

Absentmindedly, she put a finger up to touch her
lips and grinned slowly. Little by little, she was getting through to him.

He was a good guy who'd served his country. He
deserved all the happiness in the world. He'd just lost
his way and she was the one lucky enough to hold the
light for him.

Remember that, Tara. Don't get hung up on him.
You can't keep him. He's not yours for the long haul.

That was okay. She could deal with it. If she could be
an instrument in his healing, that was enough for her.

Or it would be if she just kept reminding herself
of that.

"Heads up, Duvall." Boone tossed her the keys.

She grabbed them with a one-handed catch.

He grinned. "Great reflexes."

"Thanks."

He turned to climb into the passenger seat and, as she went around to the driver's side, she swore she heard him happily humming "Everyday Is a Winding Road."

She was finally starting to get through to him. What more could a girl ask for?

THEY DROVE FOR four and a half hours.

The car should have been packed with tension after she'd kissed him, but instead, it seemed as if the kiss had actually knocked a big chunk of mortar from the emotional wall surrounding Boone.

The time flew by as they discussed everything under the sun. They talked about the best meals they'd ever eaten. For Boone, it was lobster in Maine when he'd spent a summer with his sister, Jackie, working onboard Jack Birchard's ship, the *Sea Anemone*. For Tara, it was her mother's homemade pizza.

They mused about religious beliefs and discovered that while they were both spiritual, neither was dogmatic. They were equally like-minded on politics, both holding moderate views. They talked about their favorite movies and discovered they both loved the National Lampoon vacation movies.

Boone was good company when he relaxed and they were having so much fun that Tara was startled to see the sign proclaiming Welcome to Tennessee. Wow, they were making good progress.

"I've got ancestors from Tennessee," she said.

"No kidding? Me, too. My mother's parents were originally from Knoxville."

"You're kidding? This is getting downright spooky that we have so much in common and never knew it. My kin were from Nashville."

"Anyone in your family musical?" he asked.

"Other than singing bad karaoke? Nope."

A few miles later, they drove past a mile marker that said Nashville 33 Miles and a billboard advertising the Civil War reenactment of the Battle of Shiloh for the upcoming Fourth of July weekend caught her eye.

"Ah, man," she muttered under her breath.

"What is it?" Boone asked.

"I can't believe that tomorrow is the first day of the Shiloh battlefield reenactment." She waved a hand at the billboard. "We'll be so near and I can't go."

"You're interested in battlefield reenactments?"

"My maternal great-great-great-grandfather was killed at Shiloh and I've always wanted to visit."

"It's a shame you can't go."

"So close and yet so far," she said glibly, trying to keep the wistfulness from her voice. Seeing the reenactment of the battle her ancestor had died in was on her own personal bucket list. She'd heard stories about the bravery of great-great-great-grandfather Sykes for years. His sacrifice stirred patriotism inside her. His blood traveled in hers and it made her feel connected to history in a way nothing else did.

"You really want to see the reenactment." Boone put it as a statement, not a question.

"How do you know?"

"When you want something badly, you act like you don't care."

She turned her head sharply, surprised that he'd nailed that about her.

"I've been watching you for several weeks."

"Oh, you have?" she said lightly, trying to ignore the thrill that shot through her at his admission and it was only then that she fully acknowledged how much she wanted his attention. When had this started?

"You're not fooling me one bit."

"No?"

"You act like you don't care so that if what you want doesn't happen you're not disappointed. Must come from growing up in a big family."

"You're right," she admitted. "When I was growing up, if I acted like I really wanted something, one of my older siblings would invariably get to it before I did."

"You're pretty easy to read, Duvall."

"Sorry."

"Don't be. It's not a bad thing." Boone paused. "Fact is, I wish I could be as open as you. It would make life easier."

"I think you're pretty darn terrific just the way you are," she said.

"Ditto," he said, his voice oddly husky.

Melancholy settled over her, but she batted it away. For one thing, she didn't know why she was feeling it. For another, she wasn't one to feel sorry for herself. "I really would like to see the battlefield someday."

"A guy has to be on the ball around you," he murmured.

"Oh?" She sneaked a glance over at him. His eyebrows were drawn up in a pensive expression. "What?"

"For all your openness, you're much more complex than you appear on the surface."

"Why, Boone Toliver, is that a compliment?" she teased.

"You're surprising and fun and...well...I was putting you in the same category as my mother and you don't belong there."

"No kidding," she said fiercely. "I would never ever abandon my kid. No matter what." It twisted her up inside to think of Boone as a little boy, left without a mom. It had affected him deeply, even if he didn't want to admit it. It had to have. She couldn't imagine what it was like for him, growing up knowing that your own mother didn't want you.

"You'll make a good mother someday. You'll be the cool mom and all the kids in the neighborhood will want to hang out at your house."

That pleased her. "Hey, I'm not a pushover."

"I know that. You're something else, Tara Duvall."

If, three days ago, someone had told her that she'd be in a car on her way to Miami with her grouchy neighbor and he would be saying such nice things about her, she would have laughed until her sides ached. But now? It was alarming how easily she'd grown accustomed to having him around.

Then she realized something extraordinary. She would never be the same after this road trip. Getting to know Boone on a personal level made her realize there were certain qualities she wanted in a man. Qualities she'd never searched for—or found, for that matter— before now. Boone epitomized everything she'd never known she'd wanted in a mate.

Heck, she'd never even known she was ready to start thinking about a mate until this trip.

He had his rough edges, no doubt about it, but didn't everyone? Those sharp edges and prickly patches were part and parcel of who he was. He was gruff, yes, but it was just a camouflage to hide his vulnerability, and he could admit when he was wrong. Eventually. Not easy for a strong man who was used to being in charge.

The main thing troubling him was that he hadn't found his place in the world now that he was no longer a soldier. She hoped that she was helping him with that. He seemed pretty directionless since his last knee surgery.

"So," she said. "Have you thought about what you're going to do when your knee heals?"

"*If* it heals."

"It'll heal. Third times a charm."

"You oughta find a way to bottle it."

"What?"

"That optimism of yours."

"Would you buy some if I could?"

"Maybe."

She laughed.

He scowled. "What's so funny?"

"The fact that if you could buy optimism in a bottle you're still hesitant to commit to it."

"I read a study that said pessimists have a firmer grip on reality."

"Probably, but reality is overrated."

"The study said that, too. Obviously, the paper was written by an optimist."

"You know, if I had just a few more months I bet I could turn you." Tara slipped a sideways glance at Boone.

"Turn me?"

"Into an optimist."

"You would have your work cut out for you."

"Would have been fun to try."

He was studying her intently. "I wish I'd gotten to

know you better before. I missed out on some lively conversation."

"Through no fault of my own. I tried knocking down those walls you've got built up around you, but it was a no-go."

"I should have given you a fair shake."

"As a friend?" She felt suddenly breathless, but had no idea why. Was he suggesting that if she wasn't moving to Miami there might have been something between them? But if not for this road trip they would never have gotten to know each other. Such a shame the way things turned out.

"As a better neighbor," he corrected, crushing any fantasies she once might have had about them being a couple. But hey, the door had closed on that a long time ago. Ah well, it was better this way, wasn't it?

"You never did answer my question," she said, realizing it wasn't the first time he'd avoided the topic of his future. "What *are* you going to do with yourself when you're healthy again?"

He squirmed in his seat. "Stupid knee."

She wasn't letting him off the hook with the knee excuse. "You know," she said. "I went through something similar once."

"You went through a bomb blast?"

She ignored that. "When I was eighteen and in secretarial school—"

"You were a secretary?"

"Don't sound so shocked. It's not rocket science."

"I didn't mean it that way. I just can't imagine you chained to a desk. That would be like putting a butterfly in a jar."

"Anyway, I got mono."

"That's not quite the same as going to battle."

"I know that. I'm not comparing your injury to my mono, I'm just trying to prove a point."

"Continue."

"For six weeks, all I did was sleep. My boyfriend who gave me the freaking mono dumped me—"

"What an ass."

"Thank you. I thought so, too."

"He did you a favor. You deserve better."

A sweet tingling started in her stomach, spread lower as she took in his sultry gaze. "Anyway, I also got fired from my job—"

"This was the job as the chipmunk at the amusement park?"

"Yes."

"Couldn't very well run around in a chipmunk head with mono, now, could you."

"Exactly. And I flunked out of secretarial school and had to move back home. When you're sick and all this bad stuff happens to you, it's really difficult to fight back. You start to think that this is the way your life is going to be from now on. It's easy to get depressed and not see all the joys that are waiting around the corner for you."

"You think?"

"Once I started to feel better, I began to realize something."

"What's that?"

"Getting mono was actually a real gift. I'd been studying to be a secretary to please my parents when what *I* really wanted was to style hair. So I enrolled in beauty school and the rest is history."

"Glad it worked out for you."

"Life's little detours often lead us to our real destination."

"You sound like a fortune cookie."

"Clichés are clichés for a reason."

"They're trite for a reason, too."

"I know my little story doesn't compare to all the suffering you've been through, Boone, but what I'm trying to say is that everyone comes to a crossroads in their life, and it's okay to sit and mull for a while until you figure it all out."

"I've done a helluva lot of stewing," he conceded.

"What is it you really want to do?"

"Be a soldier."

"But that path is closed. What else are you passionate about?"

"Hell if I know."

"What appealed to you about military service?"

"Knowing what's expected of you."

"You could find that in another line of work."

"Tara," he said. "I'm not you. I'm not a bright little ray of sunshine. I don't know how to pick up the pieces of my shattered life and move forward as if nothing had happened. Every minute of every day the pain reminds me of just how broken I am."

She couldn't help it—she had to peek at him. The deepening twilight cast shadows over his face. His eyes were hooded again. The scruff of stubble darkened his jaw. His breathing was ragged and she realized he'd been sitting in the passenger seat a long time without stretching his leg, and he hadn't taken a pain pill all day.

And here she'd been chattering glibly about mono. As if she could even begin to imagine the level of pain he'd suffered. Was still suffering. She could be so silly sometimes. No wonder Boone had never been her fan.

Up ahead lay an exit. Gas stations and fast food joints.

Tara did what she did best. She plastered on a happy smile, pretended everything was just fine and chirped, "Pit stop, coming right up."

9

Thursday, July 2nd, 8:52 p.m.

"I'll pump the gas," Boone offered. It was the least he could do since she was doing all the driving. She was a good sport, too, putting up with his bellyaching. He should do something nice for her. Maybe he'd buy her something special.

"You do that and I'll pop next door and grab us a bag of burgers." She nodded at the fast-food hamburger joint near the gas station. "What do you like on your burger?"

"See if they've got a salad."

"You need something more filling than a salad," she argued.

"Hey, I gotta keep a handle on my weight while I'm out of commission." He patted his belly. He might not have control over anything else, but he was determined to at least have control over his body.

Right. Good luck with that.

"I'll surprise you." She waggled her fingers at him over her shoulder.

He watched Tara walk away, hips swaying, her white

shorts showing up brightly in the dusk and felt himself harden.

Classy, Toliver. Real classy.

He just had to hang in there. They were less than a day away from Miami. By this time tomorrow they would be going their separate ways. Forever.

Why that thought ate at him, he had no idea.

That wasn't the truth. He did know why. It was because of how he felt when he was with her. Hopeful. She made him want to do better, be better.

Not to mention that she was hot as the Fourth of July rockets they were selling at the fireworks stand across the road. He should never have kissed her. Things were going along just fine until he'd kissed her in that cornfield, completely changing the sulky-war-vet-versus-sunny-ditz thing that had up until then kept them apart. When you slapped a label on someone it was easier to dismiss her, but spending this time in close proximity with Tara there was no label on earth that he could stick on her. She was unique.

He finished pumping the gas and holstered the nozzle just as Tara returned with a delicious-smelling brown paper bag.

"Guess what?" she said.

"We're going to need arterial bypasses after dinner?"

She laughed as if his joke was truly funny. "There are picnic benches and a pretty little pond behind the gas station. Let's go sit and eat. I saw lightning bugs. I love lightning bugs."

Of course she did. Lightning bugs were just like her, bright and pretty and temporary.

"This way, soldier." She headed off again, leaving him no choice but to follow her if he wanted something to eat.

He had to admit it was nice under the trees, the sound of frogs croaking, the flicker of the lightning bugs, the cool evening breeze blunting the highway noises. He sat down on the far corner of the cement picnic bench, angling his right leg out straight.

Instead of sitting across from him as he'd anticipated, Tara plunked down next to him, sitting so close he could feel her body heat. Her long, slender fingers, the nails painted a sweet salmon, unfurled the paper bag.

Disconcerted, he quickly glanced away, only to find himself peering down the V-neck of her shirt that revealed some amazing cleavage. She was just the right size. Not too big. Not too small. The size of ripe navel oranges. He loved oranges.

Purposely, he stared out across the pond. In the distance, some early fireworks popped and bright starbursts of yellow, green and red streaked into the night sky. Saturday was the Fourth of July. The day his sister, Jackie, was marrying that coastie.

"I got you a chicken wrap," Tara announced, her fingers curled around the paper-wrapped sandwich. She settled it in front of him, her graceful hand moving up the sandwich in a delicate stroke, those delectable fingers plucking at the paper as she undid the wrapping.

What was wrong with him? He was getting jacked up over a hand.

"I can unwrap it myself," he growled. "It's my knee that's out of commission, not my hands."

She raised her palms in a gesture of surrender. "Okay. Didn't mean to offend."

Crap! He'd done it again. Gotten crabby because she'd unwittingly stirred him. It wasn't her fault she was so damned sexy.

They ate in silence, watching the fireworks and the

lightning bugs, listening to the night noises and eating their sandwiches. It had been a long time since he'd had someone to share meals with and even though he was loath to admit it, he enjoyed the companionship. And she'd forgiven him again. She was munching her food with a smile on her face.

Another couple came strolling through the spot, holding hands, and they settled in at the next picnic table. They were both dressed in Civil War garb. The man was in a replica rebel uniform and the woman wore a bonnet and ankle-length calico dress.

"They must be reenactors headed for Shiloh," Tara whispered. She turned her head and the fruity scent of her hair drifted over him, enthralling him.

"How far is it from Nashville to the Shiloh battle-field?" he asked.

"A hundred miles or more."

He shifted on the bench. They were a thirty-minute drive from Nashville. At sixty miles an hour—their average speed pulling the U-Haul, a hundred miles would take them over an hour and a half. That meant it was over two hours to the Shiloh battlefield.

Tara started talking about the battle and her face lit up. Clearly, she'd done her research.

"I'm gonna go talk to them," she said, hopping up and rushing over to strike up a conversation with the couple.

Boone sat watching her. He remembered what she'd looked like coming out of the bathroom at the B&B dressed in nothing but a towel. Freaking hell, his erection was already half-mast again.

A few minutes later, she came bounding back, chattering up a storm about the reenactment. He'd never seen a woman so worked up about a battle. He got to his feet and tossed the wrapping from their sandwiches into the nearby trashcan. He wished she'd get that worked up over him.

Since when? She gets on your last nerve.

Yeah? Well that was before the trip and before he really got to know her. He swallowed his inexplicable need to kiss her again. A craving to taste those luscious lips.

This was bad news. The way she made him feel. He'd already begun projecting into the future, picturing what life would be like without her. No impromptu visits. No surprise casseroles. No funny stories or jokes. Doing something nice for her would simply make it that much harder to let go. It was better for him to keep his distance. He'd just pay a couple of hundred extra dollars. Money ought to do the trick. There was no need for him to do anything personal for her.

"You wanna go to Shiloh?" he blurted impulsively.

She blinked at him. "What?"

"You want to go watch the opening salvos? The battle starts at dawn, right?"

Pure excitement flared in her eyes. "You mean it?"

"We are this close. It would be a shame to miss it. Especially since you have a family connection."

"But what about getting to Key West in time to stop your sister's wedding?"

"It's a sixteen-hour drive from Nashville to Miami give or take. Throw in another two hours for the detour to Shiloh and two more to watch the beginning of the battle. That's twenty hours. Still time to make it to Key West by Saturday afternoon."

"Really?" She jumped up and down, a ball of exuberant energy. He'd put that expression on her face.

Boone was…well, hell…he was happy that he'd made her happy. "Sure. Why not?"

"Oh, thank you! Thank you!" She threw her arms around him and squeezed him tight. "I'm never, ever going to forget this. You're absolutely awesome."

"Which means we need to get a move on," he said, alarmed by how good it felt to be clutched in her enthusiastic embrace. "Now."

"Yes. Right. Let's go." She grabbed his hand, pulling him headlong toward the car.

Great. Now you've done it. You've bonded. You're bonding with her. You, Toliver, are sunk.

THEY REACHED THE Shiloh National Military Park just before midnight, but after an hour of checking out the local motels, they were alarmed to discover that there were no vacancies to be had. Tara hadn't even considered that.

"We can sleep in the car," Boone said, with an amazing amount of patience.

"But your leg. You need a bed to stretch out in. Maybe we could drive back to the last town and see if they have any vacancies there."

"The battle starts at dawn. It wouldn't be worth the drive back and forth for just a couple of hours' sleep. We'll be fine in the car. I can put the seat back as far as it will go."

Tara nibbled her bottom lip. She felt terrible about the motel situation. "Boone—"

"Stop over-thinking it." He yawned. "Just pull into a parking lot and let's get some shut-eye. Compared to what those Civil War soldiers went through, cramped quarters in a Honda is a luxury."

"At least take a pain pill."

When he didn't argue but pawed the pill bottle from his pocket and swallowed two with the watered-down drink left over from their previous stop, she knew he must really be hurting.

She drove into the empty parking lot of a nearby mall, and by the time she killed the engine Boone appeared to be fast asleep, his fingers interlaced, hands resting on his chest.

Hyped up about the Shiloh battlefield reenactment, it took Tara several minutes to settle down. She put her seat back and squirmed around trying to get comfortable.

She lay on her right side, hands stacked under her head, watching Boone sleep. God, he was devastatingly handsome, even when he was asleep, maybe especially when he was asleep, because there was a vulnerable air to him now that he fought hard to keep at bay when he was awake.

Her heart thumped loudly and she had no idea why. She wished she could build a wall around herself the way he did, hold her silly infatuation at bay. Why did she have to fling herself headlong into everything? Including falling for the big lug?

Tara pulled in a sigh. What was it about him that had her heart tripping all over itself?

Maybe it was the inner gentleness he tried so hard to cover up, but couldn't quite hide. Or maybe it was the way his hot eyes made her body heat up every time he looked at her, as if he'd never noticed another woman before.

A frisson of pleasure passed through her at the thought. That very well could be it.

For the longest time, she lay there, happy for a time

simply watching over him. He deserved someone to look after him. He hadn't had nearly enough of it.

She must have dozed off, because some time later something stirred her.

A throaty moan came from the other side of the car.

Boone! Something was wrong.

She jerked wide-awake and rammed her hip into the steering wheel. *Ouch!* She blinked, forgetting for a second where she was, her muscles cramped and achy.

"Get down!" Boone shouted.

Distressed, she ducked her head. Get down? What was happening? She shot a glance at the man beside her. He thrashed around in the seat, his eyes closed. "Stay back. There's a bomb!"

Tara sat up, gnawed her bottom lip. He was having a nightmare. A lump swelled in her throat. Poor guy, the horrors of the past that he hid so well while awake overcame him in slumber. His inner battle reached deep inside her, touched her soul and broke her heart.

She didn't know what to do. Should she try to rouse him? She'd heard somewhere that you shouldn't startle soldiers when they were sleeping.

"Boone," she whispered.

"No safe place," he mumbled, grunted and then winced.

Did he have post-traumatic stress disorder? It would explain a lot about him. Why he kept to himself and put up emotional barriers.

It took everything that she had in her not to touch him. "It's okay. You're not overseas. You're here, safe with me."

He shook his head. "No, no."

"Shh. Shh."

His eyes moved behind closed lids, the rapid action of dream sleep. "Tara?" he whispered hoarsely.

"Yes, I'm right here."

"Pretty Tara." His tone turned dreamy and he reached out a directionless hand, slowly pawing the air as if he were stroking her.

Oh, wow. What now?

Unexpected tingles spread throughout her body. It moved her to see him so vulnerable. It might be dangerous to wake a sleeping soldier, but she didn't feel comfortable eavesdropping on his dream apparently when he appeared to be dreaming about her now. "Boo—"

"So pretty." His hand made contact with her hair, his fingers slid through it.

His touch sent her pulse reeling. "Ah, Boone."

"I want you, Tara. I want you so bad." His eyes were opened now, but his gaze looked dazed. Was he awake or still sleeping?

Her breath slipped shallowly through her parted lips. His hand moved to cup her cheek and he slowly sat up.

"Are you awake?" she murmured.

Instead of answering, his mouth caught hers in a demanding kiss. Every muscle in her body weakened even as she willed herself not to respond. This wasn't right. Not under these circumstances. But the things he was doing to her with his tongue unraveled her completely.

"Tara," he said her name, a hot whisper in the night.

She succumbed. There was no excuse for it. She wasn't proud of herself, taking advantage of a man who might very well be sleep-kissing, but she was helpless to resist.

Dumb. Dumb. She knew it was dumb. Even if he were fully awake and in charge of everything he was doing, she should not be doing this. Because she was in danger of losing her heart to this man whom she would never see again after Saturday and if she made love to him, she feared it would seal her fate.

Whoa. Make love? You're just kissing the dude.

Yes, but she wanted to do so much more with him. Had wanted it for months. Her pulse pounded. She leaned forward, leaned into the kiss when she should be pulling away from it.

His mouth moved from her lips to kiss the underside of her jaw, turning her into liquid pools of pure heat. A soft moan slipped from her lips.

Stop it. Snap out of it.

Sounded good, but she so didn't want to. Reluctantly gathering what little sense she had left, Tara twisted away from him. "Boone, wake up."

"I'm wide-awake, sweetheart," he said, moving in to feather his tongue along the outside of her ear. "You taste delicious."

Sweetheart.

He called her sweetheart. Now she knew he had to still be asleep. Sleepy Boone might be all lovey-dovey, but Awake Boone would never call her *sweetheart*. He thought she was annoyingly cheerful. She got on his last nerve. Hadn't he told her that on more than one occasion? And yet, and yet…hadn't *something* been changing between them these last few days?

Her stomach fluttered and her fingers tangled up in his soft, shaggy hair. So easy. It would be so easy to just give in and let nature take its course. She'd been doing it all her adult life. Which was the problem. She always let life's currents carry her without much thought for the future, and so far that hadn't been such a bad thing. But she was older now and, well, she was ready for something more permanent.

Huh? When had that happened?

Probably the day she'd learned about her mother's illness. Even though her mom had an excellent chance for recovery, something like this made a girl reevaluate her life. Made her realize what really mattered.

Family.

A husband. Kids.

Struck by the revelation, she unthreaded her fingers from his hair. She hadn't even realized she was finally ready for a long-term relationship. Too bad her body ached for this short-term guy.

"Down, boy," she said, her light-hearted tone belying the crazy gallop of her thoughts. Determined to stop herself from making a big mistake, she planted both palms against his chest and immediately got snared in his dark-eyed gaze.

He searched her face and she could see he really was wide-awake. A long minute ticked between them with nothing but the sound of their heavy breathing to break the silence.

"Please…" she croaked, the word a helpless plea for him to override her objections and just kiss her again anyway.

Slowly, Boone nodded, dropped his arms and settled back into the seat.

"You were having a nightmare," she ventured.

"Yeah. I used to have them all the time in the hospital. Sorry you had to see that."

"I'm not. I'm glad."

"That I'm a monumental wreck?"

"That you're human."

He cracked a wry smile. "You had doubts?"

"C'mon. You're intimidating. Decorated war hero."

He shook his head. "It's not like you think."

"That's what I want to understand."

"War really is hell."

"Then why did you do it?"

"Somebody has to."

"You feel it's your place to clean up the world's ills?"

"Once upon a time I thought that," he said, his voice filled with regret. "But I'm older and wiser now."

She leaned over the console between them, having no real plan. She should have turned on her side in the seat, back to him and tried to sleep, but she did not. Instead, she hovered over him, almost daring him to do something about it.

Why?

The question got lost in the soft growl that escaped him as he sat up to claim her lips once more. The pressure of his diligent mouth absconded with her will, left her elated and giddy. His generous tongue eclipsed any lingering protests. Treacherously, she relished him, betraying what she knew was right.

Oh, Tara, you're so easy.

He tugged her over the console and arranged her on top of him. She straddled his waist, knees digging into the seat on either side of him. He ran his palm up the back of her neck, held her head still while he fully explored her mouth with masterful strokes.

She made a soft mewling sound and sank into him, letting go of all resistance.

His other hand tunneled between them, reaching up under the hem of her T-shirt. His knuckles skimmed her bare skin. His fingers tickled their way up. She'd slipped out of her bra before going to sleep, so there was nothing between him and her.

She shivered against him. This was exciting. She hadn't made out in a car since she was a teenager.

"Hmm." The vibration of his sound hummed against her lips.

He pushed up her shirt and slowly peeled it over her head, exposing her to the air. Then he commenced blazing a moist, deliberate trail from her lips to her throat and beyond. He cupped her breasts, weighing them in his palms. He teased one nipple with his mouth, the other with his fingers.

She squirmed, her body alive with sensation. Eager to trace the muscles, she splayed her hands under his shirt and pulled another groan from his lips when her fingers made contact with his flat belly.

Their mouths met again in a fierce clash, hungry, desperate. The same frantic way they'd kissed that first time in the Nebraska cornfield. Had it only been last night? It seemed a lifetime ago.

Through the material of his pants, she could feel him growing rock solid between her legs. Everywhere he touched her turned to liquid fire—her lips, her skin, until she was completely unbalanced. She felt as if she were falling—through time, through space, through sensation after sensation.

He sucked her nipple, his hands wrapped securely around her waist, holding her in place, keeping her steady. Balanced. He brought equilibrium into her life.

She threw back her head, arched her spine, ground herself against him until he groaned aloud.

They were lost. Carried away on lust and the sexual tension that had been mounting between them for months. Tara was ready and beside herself with desire for him.

Boone's impatient fingers plucked at the snap of her white denim shorts. She had no idea how this was going to work in the front passenger seat of her Honda, especially with him in a leg brace, but she was game to figure out the logistics. She tackled his zipper with the same gusto he went at hers.

She ached for him. Deep down. Hard and helpless. A pristine pain so sharp and pure it felt as if it could never be sated. It terrified her. This contradiction of what she wanted and what she knew was good for her. But she could not seem to swim upstream against the sexual force pushing her to merge with this man. She did not really want to resist. Not in her heart.

His hand slipped past her waistband, moved aside the skimpy material of her panties, his fingers unerringly finding her trigger. Passion seized her body, moved through her in escalating waves. She grasped both his shoulders, holding herself aloft over him while he explored her tender feminine folds.

Tara gazed down at him in the darkness that was full of shadows. His eyes were on hers. They stared at each other, into each other. His hips twitched beneath her, his erection growing harder still. His stroking escalated, stealing any rational thought. She heard a roaring in her ears, high and rough like impending rapids lying await in the next turn of a rain-swollen river.

His hand controlled her. She was a marionette and he was the puppet master, making her feel…oh, the things he was making her feel! Alive and stolen, exalted and tremulous, claimed and cherished.

Tara's blood thundered through her veins, thumped at her temples, throbbed through every cell of her body with one single word. *Boone. Boone. Boone.*

His fingers stoked her desire, stealing all thought from her head. She closed her eyes, concentrating on the amazing sensation.

"Tara" he said. "You look beautiful when you're about to come."

And she *was* about to come. Could he feel it rising up in her? Did he understand that he was her ultimate undoing?

The surge of her orgasm took her out of her body. It was a beautiful experience. She shuddered, trembled, glowed.

He had both arms around her now, pulled her protectively down onto his chest. Gently, he kissed her, his hand smoothing her sweat-dampened hair from her face. He held her while her passion dwindled and her breathing returned to normal. She couldn't help feeling guilty that she'd come alone, Boone still stalwartly in control of himself. If they hadn't been in a parked car, she would have turned the tables on him.

"Leg cramp, leg cramp," he exclaimed.

She scrambled off him and tumbled into the driver's seat, fumbling to do up her pants. "Sorry, sorry."

"Gotta stand up." He sat up and reached for the door handle.

A rap smacked against Tara's window.

The knock ricocheted around the Honda like a spent bullet. Startled, she looked over to see a uniformed Tennessee trooper standing there with an irritated scowl, just as Boone bailed out of the car.

"Got a problem here, folks?" The Tennessee state trooper shined the beam of his flashlight over them as they stood beside Tara's vehicle.

Other than the fact they'd gotten caught making out in a car? Nope. And honestly, Boone didn't even consider that a problem, because for the first time in a very long time he was enjoying himself. He grinned.

The trooper's frown deepened. "Did I say something funny?"

Tara cut her eyes at Boone. She was grinning, too.

Boone pressed his lips together, tried to stop smiling , but then he thought of how sexy Tara had looked in his lap while he'd brought her to orgasm and his lips just refused to obey and spread wide across his face once more.

"No problem here," Tara squeaked, and slammed a palm over her mouth. Her shoulders were shaking up and down.

She was laughing!

If the trooper had shown up one minute earlier, he would have caught them in a compromising position. The position he *had* caught them in was suspicious enough, but at least Tara had been dressed by then.

Boone met her gaze. She was laughing so hard that tears formed in the corners of her eyes. Her laughter caught him low in the gut and he couldn't help himself. He started laughing, too.

The trooper took a step toward them. "Are you laughing at me?"

"No, no." Tara waved a helpless hand. "Not at all." Her lively eyes drilled into Boone and her laughter swept him away. He couldn't control himself. Even in front of a ticked-off trooper, her laugh was infectious, it spread through Boone and poured from his throat in a loud guffaw.

"Stop laughing!" the trooper commanded.

Tara tried to force herself to sober. She turned her mouth down, made her expression solemn and looked away from Boone.

"Leg cramp," Boone whispered to her mischievously.

Tara broke into fresh gales of laughter and Boone joined in.

"Are you folks interested in spending the night in lockup?" the trooper threatened. "'Cause that's where you're headed."

"We're sorry, Officer," Boone said. "We just got carried away by the situation."

The trooper rested his hands on his hips. "Most people don't laugh when they get stopped by law enforcement." He took another step closer to Boone. "You been drinking?"

Tara put a hand up. "We're sorry, we're sorry. We've been driving for hours and just got the giggles. We haven't been drinking. And as you can see—" she waved a hand at the brace on Boone's knee "—he hasn't been driving."

"You willing to take a sobriety test?"

Boone notched up his chin. "I am."

"He hurt his knee in Afghanistan," Tara said. "Defending our country."

The trooper's face softened. "That true?"

"It is."

"What branch of service?"

"Army. Green Beret."

The trooper looked suitably impressed. "My brother served over there. I have some small inkling of what you went through. You will get settled again. Don't give up. It's not as dark as it seems."

Boone glanced at Tara. "I'm starting to see a light at the end of the tunnel."

"Thank you for your sacrifice."

"Thank you," Boone said, because he didn't know what else to say.

"Listen," the trooper said, "you can't stay here, but

there's a store up the road. They don't mind if people camp out in their parking lot."

"Thank you, Officer. We're sorry for the inconvenience," Tara said.

"Take good care of him," the trooper told Tara. "He needs your love and support right now."

"I'm doing my best."

Boone's heart did a crazy dip and swirl.

The trooper tipped his hat. "You folks have a good night."

He headed for his patrol car and they got back into the Honda.

"Wow," Tara said. "That was a close one."

"It was."

"I can't believe we got the giggles."

"Bad timing."

"You made it worse by saying 'leg cramp.' That was the last thing I expected from you."

"I know." He smiled. "That's why I did it."

"Oh, Boone Toliver." She grinned and started the engine. "You're turning out to have quite the sense of humor."

And as she drove back onto the road, Boone realized that he couldn't remember the last time he'd felt so good.

10

THEY MANAGED TO SNAG a few hours of sleep in the car in the parking lot of the nearby store, and after they woke up, they had breakfast at a nearby pancake house. They'd changed clothes and freshened up in the restaurant's restroom and then drove to Shiloh National Military Park, arriving a few minutes before the 6:00 a.m. start time.

The troops were in place, cannons and horses at the ready, blue on one side, gray on the other. Tara stood on tiptoes to see over the head of the tourist standing in front of her.

Boone slipped a hand around her waist and she leaned against him, inhaling the cottony scent of his shirt. Something had changed in him—changed between them. It was more than just what had happened earlier in the intimacy of her car, but Tara couldn't put her finger on what it was exactly.

"I'm glad you're here with me," she said. "This wouldn't be nearly as much fun by myself."

"Me, too. I can't think of anyone I'd rather see the Battle of Shiloh with."

"Wouldn't one of your old war buddies be a better choice? You could talk battlefield strategy and they'd understand."

"You sell yourself short. Besides, none of my old buddies smell as good as you do." He grinned.

"Remind me to buy more green-apple shampoo."

"Ah, so that's what it is. Green apples."

She could feel the heat of his gaze on her face. A cannon shot went off. Tara jumped. The odor of gunpowder stirred the air. "The battle is starting."

"Uh-huh." He didn't look out across the field. He was totally fixed on her.

Unsettled by his attention, Tara's cheeks warmed and she felt suddenly embarrassed under his scrutiny. "The rebels are making their move." She pointed out the advancing regiment, eager to get him to look at something besides her.

Finally, thankfully, Boone shifted his gaze to the battlefield.

Cameras flashed and cell phones clicked as the crowd snapped photographs and took videos grounding the surreal depiction of the past in modern day reality. People were texting, posting to Facebook and Tweeting the event.

"Wonder what my great-great-great-grandfather would have thought of the twenty-first century Shiloh," she mused to Boone.

"No doubt he'd be stunned by the changes of a hundred and fifty years."

"I can't imagine it."

"What was his name?"

"Travis Sykes. He's a legend in our family. According to the story, he'd died saving the lives of two other men. One of them survived the war and when it was over, he went to pay his respects to my great-great-great-grandmother Matilda and ended up marrying her."

"Ouch. Kick in the teeth to poor Travis. Save the guy and he ends up bedding your wife."

"It wasn't like that. Not at all. Both Matilda and Richard—that was my step-great-great-great-grandfather's name—had a deep reverence for Travis and the sacrifices he made. Richard married Matilda as a way to pay back the life Travis had given him. Those kids needed a daddy."

"That's the kind of stuff of Hollywood love stories. They could make a movie about it."

"Not really. Turns out Matilda and Richard really weren't too fond of each other. They used to have the worst knock-down drag-out fights, but they both respected Travis and so they stayed together out of misguided loyalty or maybe it was simply a sign of their times. People just didn't get divorced back then. My family tends to downplay that part of the story."

"Still, it's pretty impressive that your family has kept Travis's legacy alive all these years. It's something most soldiers only dream of."

"Does it make you sad?" she asked.

He frowned. "What?"

"That you don't have anyone to keep your legacy alive?"

He shifted. Favoring his leg? Or had her question made him uncomfortable? "I've got a sister—"

"Who currently isn't speaking to you, plus it sounds like she has plenty of legacy of her own since her father is a renowned oceanographer."

"Trying to stir up trouble, Duvall?" The corners of his mouth quirked, letting her know that he wasn't really irritated.

"It's just…well…you're all alone in that house since your dad died."

"And?"

"Nothing. Never mind." What Boone did with his life was none of her business, but it made her sad to think that he didn't have a family to pass along his legacy.

"It's impossible to stop you from worrying about other people, huh?" His voice was tenderly rough.

She canted her head, grinned up at him. "Yeah."

"You've got a good heart, Tara."

His compliment bowled her over. She wished she could read something more into it, but she didn't dare. They had no future. No point dreaming up fantasies. Once they were in Miami, he'd be out of her life for good.

"Nice day for a gory reenactment." She changed the subject.

"Yes, but I don't like the looks of those clouds." He nodded toward the north.

Sure enough, a bank of dark clouds, while providing a nice respite from the heat, were beginning to close in.

Tara shivered. Storms made her nervous. "Villainous skies."

"We'll be driving in it."

"Maybe not," she replied and resolved not to worry about the impending rain. Why borrow trouble when the storms could just as easily pass them by?

More people arrived, pushing the crowd in the viewing area closer together. Boone stepped behind Tara, his big strength looming over her, causing her to feel incredibly safe and protected. She liked the feeling far more than she should have.

Stop idealizing him.

Then he did something that took her totally by surprise. He put his arms around her shoulders and drew her against him, the weight of his arms resting comfortably on her collarbones, his broad chest pressed against her spine. The close contact sent waves of pleased satisfaction rippling through her.

They watched in silence for the next hour as the battle played out before them. History came alive. The crowd had fallen into hushed reverence. Tara put herself on the battlefield, imaging she was great-great-great-grandfather Travis. He'd only been twenty-three, two years younger than she was now. He must have been so scared.

Soldiers paid such a high price defending those at home. Boone, too, had paid dearly for his country. Standing this close to him, thinking about all he'd suffered, plucked at her heartstrings and muddled her brain.

As if sensing her tension, Boone tightened his arm around her neck, a reassuring gesture that touched something deep inside her. They'd made a connection, this morning, last night, at the firing range and in that Nebraska cornfield. The roots of it had started before that, even though she imagined Boone would deny it.

"We better go," she said, realizing he'd been standing for almost two hours on that wounded leg. But she didn't want to call attention to his weakness, so she nodded at the gray sky clotted with buttermilk clouds. "Get a head start on that rain."

"You sure you don't want to stay a little longer?" he offered. "It's just now eight."

"I appreciate the offer, but we're still sixteen hours out of Miami."

"Which puts us there at around midnight."

"If we drive straight through."

"Even with a couple of short stops we should still get to Miami by one or two tomorrow morning."

"Don't forget you still have to get from Miami to Key West. That's a two-hour drive without traffic, and you'll need to sleep at least a few hours. We didn't sleep much last night."

"Are you sure?" He waved at the battlefield. "You may never get up here again."

"This sojourn is enough. I can cross it off my bucket list."

"If you're sure…"

"I am." She moved to take his hand, and to Tara's pleasure, he let her.

SOMETHING HAD STARTED changing in Boone even though he couldn't say what it was. Instead of being quiet and circumspect, he found himself wanting to tell Tara everything about himself. Which was odd. He'd never been the kind of guy to easily share secrets. When he was being self-aware—which he usually tried to avoid at all costs—he had to admit that his silence had been just as much an issue in his marriage as Shaina's fickleness. He had to admit that she hadn't known what she was signing up for when she married him because he hadn't allowed her to really know him.

But now here he was, yakking up a storm like he and Tara were fast friends and he couldn't strip himself bare fast enough as they rolled south. He glanced over at her. She was the most gorgeous thing—all blonde and sexy and fun. No wonder everyone loved her.

They drove through Tennessee and passed along the Smoky Mountains. The scenery was breathtaking. Tara told him she'd taken banjo lessons when she was ten, but turned out to be hopeless at it. Boone confessed his father had coaxed him into taking guitar lessons, but he'd been equally unsuccessful.

They stopped for gas and had pulled-pork sandwiches for lunch at a little out-of-the-way place that had rocking chairs on the front porch. Tara looked completely surprised when he asked if she wanted to sit on the porch and rock and look at the mountains for a few minutes before they hit the road again.

"Really? Can we spare the time after we stopped in Shiloh?"

"Just for a few minutes," he said, surprised that he wanted to linger here with her.

There was a checkerboard set up between two rockers. "Interested in a game?" he asked.

Her jaw dropped. "What have you done with Boone Toliver?"

"He's taken the day off."

"Hmm, I like this hooky-playing Boone. But really, do we have time?"

"I'm a whiz at checkers. I'll beat your pants off in nothing flat."

"What girl could resist a challenge like that? Having the pants beat off of her by a Green Beret. You're on."

The pit stop ended up taking over an hour, but by the time they got back into the car, Boone was so relaxed he wished they could have spent the entire day on that porch.

Once they were on their way, he dozed off and woke with a start two hours later.

"Where are we?" He yawned. Stretched.

"Georgia."

"Sorry to fall asleep on you."

"Don't be. You needed it."

"So do you."

"I'll have plenty of time to sleep after I get you to Key West."

When he was no longer around. Disappointment kicked him in the gut. He was going to miss her.

They took another quick bathroom break and Tara bought a sack of peaches at a roadside stand. The scent from the fruit filled the car.

"Yum," she said, taking a bite as she started the car once more. "Juicy."

"Just like you."

"Boone! Are you flirting with me?"

"Did I say that out loud?"

"You did." She gave him a sexy look and tossed him the peach. "Nibble on this. It will have to do until you can nibble on me."

Adrenaline sped a dose of excitement through Boone's bloodstream. He thought about last night. How his recurring nightmare had shifted to an erotic dream about Tara, and then he'd awakened in the middle of it to find himself kissing her. Damn his foolish hide, he'd gone with it. Just like he was going with this teasing high-speed flirtation. He was out of his league here. She possessed a master wit.

"These are freestone peaches," she said. "They're juicier than cling peaches, so because of that they're better for eating. But they disintegrate when you cook with them, so cling peaches are better for cooking."

"How do you know that?"

"Trial and error. The first time I made peach cobbler I used freestone and ended up with little more than peach flavored dough. What about you? You ever made peach cobbler?"

"No, but I made an apple pie once. For my ex-wife."

"Really? How did that go?"

"Not well. I think I overcooked the apples. Do they have freestone apples? Maybe that's what I did wrong."

"No freestone apples as far as I know."

"I cheated," he confessed.

"On your ex-wife?"

"On the pie."

"How's that?"

"I used premade pie crust. My ex complained about it."

"Hey, if a guy went to all the trouble to make me a pie, I wouldn't make a peep about the crust."

"Good to know."

The closer they got to Miami, the more he talked. He seemed compelled to tell her as much as possible about himself before he ran out of time.

They talked about childhood memories. Hers included tales of gator hunting and jaunts on swamp boats with her uncle. His memories entailed horseback riding and fly-fishing. They talked about vacations they'd taken and movies they'd seen. No surprise there that she liked romantic comedies while he preferred thrillers.

"Favorite music?" she asked.

"Country and western. You?"

"Alternative rock." She plucked another peach from

the sack they'd gotten at a roadside stand. She took a bite of the plump, orange fruit and juice dribbled down her chin.

Boone passed her a napkin. Laughing, she dabbed the juice away.

"You know," she said, "I thought this trip was going to be a living hell, but I'm actually having fun."

"Living hell, huh?"

She shrugged, chewing her peach pensively. "Admit it, you're not the most pleasant person in the world."

"I thought you liked me."

"No…" She paused, took another bite. "I felt sorry for you."

That hurt his feelings a little, but he wasn't going to let her know it.

"But I like you now," she rushed to add. "Well and truly. You're not as much of a sourpuss as you like people to believe."

Was he really that off-putting to people? "Hey, I wasn't looking forward to this trip any more than you were."

"But you got over it." She turned to beam at him. "I'm irresistible."

"And humble."

She stuck her tongue out at him. Grinned.

Ah, her sweet, pink, industrious tongue. "Storm's rolling in faster than I expected," he said, but he wasn't looking at the sky. All his attention was focused on Tara.

"Coming on strong."

"Force of nature. It's gonna hit hard and wet."

"I could try to outrun it." She pressed her foot down on the accelerator and the car shot forward.

"You can run but you can't hide."

"Cliché," she said.

"You were the one who said clichés were clichés for a reason," he pointed out.

"This one is a false cliché. Of course you can hide. We could pull under a gas station awning and wait out the storm. That would be the equivalent of hiding."

"Maybe, for a little while. But eventually what you're running from will catch up to you."

"Like the fact that you're never going to be a soldier again."

"I thought we were flirting here, and you have to bring in the downer."

"Sorry. Poor form. Let's get back to the banter. Where were we?"

"Too late now." He gave her a smile, but it was true, the light-hearted mood had been pushed out by the storm.

Fat drops of rain splattered against the windshield and the late afternoon sky behind them quickly turned the color of a bruise—green, purple and deep, dark blue. Trees whipped in the gusting wind. Boone leaned over and switched on the radio, searched for a weather report.

"The fierce line of squalls pushing up from Texas is spreading across the south with thirty-mile-an-hour winds with possible hail. Reports of tornado sightings have cropped up from Arkansas to Alabama. The storms are expected to last well into early Saturday morning. If you don't have to travel in this mess, don't."

"Fudge crackers," Tara exclaimed and grasped the steering wheel tighter.

"What town is coming up next?" he asked.

Tara punched the map on the GPS. "The Florida border is coming up in just a couple of miles."

"We need to stop and let these storms pass."

"We're still seven hours from Miami."

"Can't keep driving in this storm. Pull over at the next motel you find. We can get some sleep and try again when the storms pass."

"Are you sure? I don't mind driving in it," she said, but her voice was high and reedy.

He could let her drive on or he could take a stand. He knew she was trying to make up time to thank him for the detour to Shiloh, and he didn't miss the fact that she kept restlessly bouncing her left leg up and down. She was nervous. "Get off the highway as soon as you can."

Tara looked like she was about to argue, but then a wild gust of wind hit the car. Her face paled and she pulled her bottom lip up between her front teeth. "Whoa, okay, I'm convinced. Keep your eyes peeled for the next exit."

They found a modestly priced motel and pulled into the parking lot. The rain doused them in an unforgiving deluge. Tara did not sprint ahead of Boone for the shelter of the lobby, even though her heart was pounding and fear had a choke hold on her throat. She'd never quite conquered her fear of thunderstorms.

Instead, she forced herself to match his faltering steps as he hobbled into the motel. His face was stony, but she could tell the knee was bothering him. Sleeping in the car hadn't done him any favors. No matter how much he tried to deny it, the trip had been hard on him. Hopefully, the storm would soon pass.

Tara stood shivering at the front desk. While Boone

took out his wallet, water dripped off her, pooled on the pink-and-green linoleum floor. She wrapped her arms around her and clamped her jaw tight to keep her teeth from chattering.

"Two rooms," Boone told the thin-faced young clerk whose nametag read Raj.

Raj shook his head. "One room only."

"We need two rooms."

"The storm has filled us up. We have one room left."

Boone shot a glance at Tara.

"One room is fine," she said sensibly. "We'll only be here until the storm passes."

Raj pressed his lips together in a solemn expression. "The storms will not abate for many hours."

"Maybe it won't be as bad as the weather bureau claims."

"The room has a single queen-sized bed," Raj warned.

"There's absolutely nothing else?" Boone asked.

"Get the room," Tara reiterated, even as trepidation lifted the hairs on her arms. Share a bed with Boone? She gulped. "We're lucky to get here when we did or we'd be spending another night in the car."

Boone grunted at that prospect and exchanged cash for two room keys. Raj gave him a conspiratorial wink.

"We're traveling companions, not lovers," Tara blurted, then immediately wondered why she felt obligated to say that.

"Of course not," Raj said coolly and winked at Boone again.

"We're *not*."

Boone gripped her arm.

"Seriously, sir, there's no need for winking." Tara couldn't seem to stop blathering. Damn her tendency to babble when she was nervous, and it wasn't just the gathering storm that had unsettled her. "We're not lovers."

"At least not yet." Raj nodded knowingly. "After one night sharing the same bed, who knows? Cupid works in mysterious ways."

"We're—"

The wind snatched up her protest as Boone hauled her from the lobby.

Their room was at the far end of the building, accessible only through the parking lot, which meant another foray back into the dark, rainy night. Tara swallowed bravely and struggled not to let on exactly how scared she was, by the prospect of sleeping with Boone and by the escalating storm. By the time they were settled in the room it was almost 7:00 p.m.

"We're soaked," Tara proclaimed.

"You can have the bathroom," Boone said. "I'll get on the phone and see if I can find someone to deliver us food."

Tara nodded, suddenly feeling very self-conscious. The wind rattled the windowpanes, underscoring her growing anxiety. She hoisted her overnight bag onto her shoulder, went into the bathroom and closed the door behind her. She couldn't help thinking about the last room they'd been in together at the Rose Garden B&B in Nebraska. Already, it seemed so long ago. Her relationship with Boone had come a long way since then. He'd opened up to her, relaxed, let down his guard and that was a huge step for him. When he'd suggested lingering on the porch for a game of checkers, she'd been completely bowled over.

She showered, shampooed and got out of the tub. After toweling herself dry, she put on a pair of Lycra yoga pants, a white T-shirt and flip-flops, and then wove her hair into a tidy braid. She took her time, prolonging the moment when she would have to join Boone again. Until she realized she was being selfish by hogging the bathroom.

"Okay, Miss Piggy," she scolded her reflection, as she twisted the end of her braid with an elastic tie. "Time to face the music."

It wasn't until then that she understood how tense she was about being alone with Boone, which was odd when she thought about it, since they'd been alone in the car for hundreds of miles. But things had taken a sharp turn between them last night and, well…she couldn't help thinking about how tough it was going to be to say goodbye. Especially since they hadn't had an opportunity to fully explore what was happening between them.

"That's a good thing," she assured herself, but she couldn't help feeling strangely disappointed.

She opened the door and stepped back into the motel room. It was clean, but nothing fancy. Boone sat at the utilitarian desk, his leg propped up on a second chair. The garish gold bedspread had been removed, folded and put on the dresser. On the bed lay a plethora of vending-machine food—peanuts and potato chips, cellophane-wrapped ham-and-cheese sandwiches, bagged popcorn, Oreo cookies and Twizzlers.

"No one would deliver in this storm," Boone apologized. "So I cleaned out the vending machine."

"Hey." Tara grinned. "I love junk food." She reached for one of the sandwiches.

"You're not afraid of food poisoning?"

"This sucker doesn't expire for another week." She showed him the date on the package. "And I've got a cast-iron stomach." Cheerfully, she unwrapped the sandwich, happy to have something to focus on besides how sexy Boone looked with his thick, rain-dampened hair swept back off his forehead.

"Toss me one of those sandwiches," he said. "If you're going to live dangerously, I might as well keep you company."

She underhanded the sandwich and he caught it with an easy lift of his hand. Snap. Grab. Tara bounced up on the middle of the bed and sat cross-legged amidst the snacks. She took a bite of the sandwich. Chewed.

"Not the best ham-and-cheese sammie I ever had," she observed. "Bread's soggy. But not the worst, either."

"What was the worse?" Boone asked, leaning over to reach for a package of barbecued chips.

"Kiosk at an airport terminal in Mexico. The bread was three days' worth of stale and the cheese was hard. I ate it anyway." Tara shrugged. "Didn't kill me."

"Whereabouts in Mexico?"

"Cancun. One of those crazy spring-break trips you try to forget."

"Girls Gone Wild, huh?" Boone stared at her through half-closed eyes.

Her cheeks heated. "Not quite that gutsy. No free boob shots for any twerp with a camera, but I have done my share of partying too hardy. I figure you're only young and dumb once, right?"

"You gotta be careful out there," he said. "The world is a dangerous place. I bet you gave your parents ulcers."

"Probably," she said and tore into a package of cheese puffs. She popped a couple into her mouth, her fingers instantly orange.

"You're too damned cute for my own good," Boone mumbled.

"What?"

"How 'bout we check on the weather?" He picked up the television remote and switched on the old-fashioned tube TV sitting on the scarred wardrobe. He flipped through the channels until he found a weather report. The screen depicted a steady, dark-red line of thunderstorms whirling toward the eastern seaboard. Boone blew out his breath.

"Don't fret. You've still got until four tomorrow afternoon to make it to Key West."

"Which is still about eight hours away, give or take."

"So the drop-dead time we need to leave here is—"

"No later than eight tomorrow morning."

"That's still eleven hours away. The storm is bound to pass by then," she said in her best cheerleader tone, even though the Doppler radar on TV belied her assertion. At the picture of angry clouds marching toward them, her stomach pitched.

A long moment passed as they finished eating, neither of them saying anything. Then finally, Boone said, "Tara, what if I don't make it to Key West in time?"

"You'll make it," she insisted.

"But what if I don't?"

"Then your sister will get married without you being there."

He winced. "What if this guy is totally wrong for her?"

"It's up to her to figure that out, Boone."

"It'd kill me to see her go through a divorce."

"Don't borrow trouble. Have a little faith in your sister. Maybe this guy she's marrying is the absolutely right one for her and you'll arrive to find her deliriously happy and you guys can have a heartfelt reunion."

"I can only hope."

Tara dusted the cheese puff from her fingers, hopped

off the bed and went over to put a hand on his shoulder. "Things turn out the way they're supposed to."

"You really believe that?"

"Try as you might, you can't control every outcome."

His muscles tensed under her touch. "I need a shower," he said and abruptly got up.

Tara watched him limp away from her and wondered exactly what she'd said wrong.

11

BOONE WAS RATTLED. Tara had done nothing more than put a hand on his shoulder in a sympathetic gesture and he'd immediately gotten aroused. He wasn't proud of his lack of self-control, but there it was. Whenever he was around her, he turned into a chest-thumping caveman. If he were being honest with himself, he'd admit she'd gotten to him long before the road trip.

"Doesn't matter," he growled under his breath. "She's starting over in Miami, you live in Bozeman." Yet he couldn't help feeling foolish that he'd kept her at a distance these past months. If he'd known then what he knew now...

Well, that was all water under the damn bridge, wasn't it? Besides, what did he have to offer a woman like her? He was busted both mentally and physically. Except whenever he was around her, he couldn't help feeling hopeful again and that was a very scary thing.

He wanted her so badly he could taste it. Last night, in his sleep, he'd crossed a line and when he'd awakened to find himself kissing her, he'd just gone with it.

Huge mistake. He hadn't been able to keep his mind off her all day. Worse, he hadn't wanted to keep his mind off her.

"All you gotta do is hold out for a few more hours."

Easy to say, but he was going to have to crawl into that bed and spend the night beside her.

You can always sleep on the floor.

His knee ached at the thought.

You can handle this. It's just one night. You can get through it. Yes, okay, she's impossibly sexy, but you've got a bum leg. How much could you do, anyway?

He should never have issued himself that challenge, because his mind immediately conjured up a dozen different ways of working around his injury.

"Stop it," he said aloud to his reflection in the mirror. "You're keeping a tight rein on your sex drive come hell or high water."

From the sound of the rain pounding on the roof that might be one helluva chore.

TARA FLIPPED THROUGH the channels while she listened to Boone moving around in the bathroom. Her wicked mind's eye kept imagining what he looked like naked.

He's off-limits. Out of bounds. Even if you're up for a casual fling, he's not.

How was she going to make it through an entire night lying next to him in a soft, cushy bed? Last night had been risky enough in the front seat of her Honda. What if he talked in his sleep?

"You're not going to get a lick of sleep," she mumbled. Oh well, soon enough they'd be in Miami and Boone would be out of her life for good. She felt relieved and saddened in equal measures.

The shower came on, and immediately the visions of a naked Boone bounced back into her head.

Anxious for something to distract her, she turned on the television, found a classic movie channel. *It Happened One Night* was on. Perfect. She plumped up the pillows and lay back against the headboard. When the bathroom door clicked opened, she pretended to be completely engrossed in Clark Gable and Claudette Colbert's banter. It was the scene where Clark appropriates Claudette's money on the bus—and here she thought Boone was high-handed.

Still, she couldn't help sliding a sideways glance in Boone's direction. His shaggy hair was slicked back on his forehead and gleamed wetly in the glare of the overhead light. He wasn't wearing the knee brace, and for the first time she saw his naked damaged leg.

Tara gave up pretending to watch the movie as she took in the ravaged landscape of Boone's leg. A fresh, angry purple-red scar curved around his swollen kneecap like a maniacal smile, but beyond that was a railroad of other scars in various stages of fading. Three surgeries. He'd had three surgeries to repair his knee and each had taken their toll. Sympathy was a boulder in her throat.

"Don't," he warned.

"What?"

"Don't feel sorry for me."

"I'm not."

"Don't lie. I can see it in your eyes. It's the same look that you had in your eyes when that baby squirrel fell out of the tree in your front yard and you brought it across the street to ask me for my help."

"That was really nice of you, by the way. A lot of

guys would have told me I was silly for getting so upset over a baby squirrel."

He shrugged. "All I did was call the wildlife service."

"No," she said. "You did much more than that. You took me seriously and because of you, Violet lived."

"You named her?"

"Sure, she made an impression on me."

"You're too soft-hearted, Tara."

"Don't pretend you're not. You're the one who got Violet to take milk through an eyedropper until the wildlife vet tech could come pick her up. I can still see you cupping that tiny little squirrel in your hand. You're not as big a badass as you want everyone to believe."

He cocked his head and gave her such a stunning smile that it took her breath. He didn't smile often, but when he did his face transformed from ruggedly good-looking into devastatingly handsome. He turned his attention to the television set. "Watchya watching?"

"It Happened One Night."

"Never heard of it."

"Honestly?" She stared at him, incredulous. "It's a road trip classic romance."

"Oddly appropriate." He gestured at the screen where Clark Gable was stringing up a blanket to divide the cabin in half. "Should we try that?"

"It was a very risqué movie for its time," Tara explained.

"Still feels sexually charged," he commented, but his eyes were on her, not the movie.

"Popcorn?" Wide-eyed, Tara tore open the bag of vending-machine popcorn and offered it to him.

He held up a hand. "I'm good."

Gingerly, he eased down on the far edge of the bed, the mattress dipping under his weight. Tara tensed, kept her gaze trained on the TV but she didn't hear a word. Who cared what was going on between Clark and Claudette when her own body was so aroused?

His scent drifted over to her. Cedar-scented soap. Citrusy shampoo. Spearmint toothpaste. Clean and fresh and perfect.

Being here with him felt too intimate. Too dangerously close to something meaningful. Clark Gable's idea of dividing the room with a blanket seemed more and more appealing. Except if Boone wanted her, no amount of material would hold him back.

Tara gulped, aware of just how powerfully masculine he was. She was just about to change the channel when lightning flashed outside the window and suddenly the TV went off.

"Looks like we lost the cable."

"We've still got the lights," she said optimistically and hopped off the bed. She felt too edgy to keep sitting there. How in the heck was she supposed to last the night alone in the bed with him without even the TV for distraction?

Thunder crashed. Tara jumped.

"You okay?"

"Storms make me nervous," she admitted.

"Try to relax."

Relax? How could she relax in a room with a man whose bones she ached to jump? A man who, if she was being honest with herself, she cared about far more than was wise. How could she be calm when a storm raged both inside and out?

More lightning, forked and vividly close, flashed outside the window. Thunder shook the windowpanes.

Tara paced the room, then realized her breasts were

bouncing underneath her T-shirt and Boone had noticed. She stopped, crossing her arms over her chest.

"What calms you down?" he asked.

She bit down on her tongue to keep from saying "sex." This was not the time to poke the lazy blaze building inside her.

Boone's hair fell over his forehead and he stabbed it back with his fingers.

"You know," she said, "cutting hair relaxes me. I could give you a haircut so you don't have to show up at your sister's wedding looking like a Wookiee."

"If I ever get there," he grumbled. "This trip has been one long delay after another. The storm seems to be getting worse instead of easing up."

"Now who needs to relax?"

"You're right. I am uptight."

"Understatement of the century," she mumbled under her breath.

"I heard that."

"Maybe the storm is fate's way of trying to tell us something."

"Yeah? And what would that be?"

"That you shouldn't interrupt your sister's wedding plans."

"I don't believe in fate."

"Doesn't matter."

"What doesn't?"

"It doesn't matter if you believe in fate or not. Fate believes in you, and don't roll your eyes."

His smile was mild. "You're starting to know me too well, Tara."

"So, you wanna haircut or what?"

"Why don't we just hit the sheets?"

The word *sheets* sent a sweet shiver up her spine. She ignored that and said, "Let me just get my scissors."

"It's late."

"Not even ten o'clock."

"We're both exhausted."

"Won't take me ten minutes."

"The storm has got you jumpy."

"I'm a professional. I promise I won't snip off your ear." She fished around in her overnight bag.

"You carry scissors in your overnight bag?"

"Never know when someone might need a haircut." She pulled a comb and styling scissors from her bag, slipped the scissors from their carrying case. "Let's do this in the bathroom so we don't get hair on the rug." She grabbed the straight-back desk chair and dragged it into the bathroom.

Reluctantly, Boone got up off the bed and followed her. He settled into the chair in front of the bathroom mirror. She draped a bath towel around his shoulders.

"Just take a little off the top—"

"Who's the stylist here?"

"You are."

"So just let me do my thing. I've got the perfect style for you."

"That's a scary thought."

"What? You don't trust me?"

"Hey, two months ago *you* had purple hair."

"Don't worry, I won't give you purple hair."

"I'm just teasing," he said. "I know you're good at your job."

His compliment pleased her. "Why, thank you. Now hold your head still." She cupped his chin, soft from where he'd shaved off the scruff of beard, and tilted it where she wanted it. "There."

She rested one hand on his shoulder, disconcerted by the strange pounding of her heart. His muscles were so firm and she was standing so close to him. Determinedly, she shook off her awareness of him and ran the comb through his silky dark hair. Cutting his hair seemed way too familiar and she couldn't help feeling she'd crossed some kind of invisible line. Moving from merely neighbors to…what? Not friends. What she felt for him was far beyond friendly, but there was no sense in becoming lovers. Not now. Not at this late date.

Why not? He's the perfect person to have a one-night stand with. No hurt feelings. No consequences.

Except Tara knew that was absolutely not true. Over the course of the last few days she'd come to truly like Boone. She'd already respected and admired him for his service to his country, but now she knew his secrets and he knew hers. It made them both too vulnerable. They could hurt each other really badly.

"You smell nice," Boone said, jerking her from her thoughts.

"What?"

"You smell like flowers. Purple ones."

"I use lavender body spray."

"It's nice."

"Thank you," she said awkwardly and concentrated on measuring his hair between her fingers. She was completely aware of everything about him, from the razor-straight set to his shoulders, to biceps big and hard as hammers, to his broad, tanned back. How did he stay so tanned when he'd been in and out of the hospital for months?

The scissors made snipping noises in the quiet room punctuated only by the sounds of their tandem raspy breathing and the thunder's frequent rumble. She realized now why she'd offered to cut his hair. It was to delay slipping between the covers with him, knowing it was their last night together. A sensible woman would keep her hands to herself.

But Tara did not want to keep her hands to herself, ergo the problem, and touching his hair, instead of sating her need as she'd hoped, inflamed it. Halfway through the haircut, she sorely regretted her offer, but she was stuck. Couldn't leave the man half-shorn.

He smelled so good that it was all she could do to keep from leaning over and planting a kiss on the nape of his neck. She finished up her task as quickly as she could, managing to fight off her impulses with the last thread of control she possessed.

"There," she said, dusting off his shoulders with the towel and stepping away.

Boone stood up. The bath towel was still wrapped around his waist and he stepped to the mirror to examine the haircut. Tara bent to pick up the hair that had fallen to the floor, but she couldn't help glancing up at him.

"Great job." He raised both hands up to thread them through his hair, but as he did so, the towel tied at his waist popped loose, giving Tara a glimpse of the most spectacular set of buns she'd ever seen.

Just as the lights winked out.

Boone froze.

Had she seen anything before the lights went out? He gulped, intimidated. Hell, he'd gone through a war, survived three knee surgeries and lost his dad. But none of those things intimidated him like being naked in the dark, alone with Tara.

The room was totally black, telling him the power

was out all over. She didn't say a word. In fact, he couldn't even hear her breathing. It was an eerie feeling. "Tara? You okay?"

"Fine and dandy," she said with that optimistic chirp he loved about her. "I'm afraid to move in case I run into something. I have a terrible sense of direction in the dark."

He reached out a hand and found her shoulder. "I'm here." *Naked.*

Tara hissed in a breath.

Boone didn't know what to do. Should he try to reach down and feel around for his towel? Should he guide her toward the bed?

Tara trembled beneath his touch. "I'm terrified of tornadoes. I lost my uncle in the Joplin tornado. Actually, I'm scared of storms altogether."

"And yet you drove in one?"

"I was trying to get you to Miami as fast as I could. I made you a promise and I live up to my promises."

"Come hell or high water?"

"You got it."

It hit Boone then, hard as a sucker punch. That she'd been willing to drive through a thunderstorm for him when she was afraid of the damn things. A warm sensation poured through him. Then he did the dumbest thing he'd ever done in his life. He pulled her into his arms.

And she let him.

He tugged her tight into the crook of his arm. "It's okay. You're safe here with me."

Then she completely knocked the pins out from under him by resting her head on his shoulder. When she wrapped her arms around his waist, he was down for the count.

He stiffened—thrilled and elated and scared and nervous. His heart was thumping and his mouth was dry and his chest tightened. He wanted her. Desperately. And the depth of his need scared the hell out of him.

Unable to resist, Boone slowly lowered his head and kissed the top of her head.

Tara tightened her arms around him, tilted her face up.

He took her lips. Gently. Sweetly. She tasted like the most decadent of desserts—impossibly sweet and hopelessly addicting. When her smart little tongue darted out to touch his, he felt as if he'd been given the keys to heaven.

Pulling her closer to him, he deepened the kiss. She made a sexy noise of approval that stroked a groan of pleasure from him. She was soft in all the right places and he was hard as a brick. There was no mistaking the strength of his desire for her.

Her warm sigh of delight sent a rush of emotion charging through him. Emotions he did not remember ever having experienced. Not with Shaina. Not with any woman.

She reached up to cup his cheek with her palm in such a tender gesture his heart skipped a beat. He knew this was dangerous, but he could not seem to stop himself. He wasn't the type to rush headlong into something, but here he was, rushing faster than a speeding roller coaster.

For most of his life, he'd been a soldier. It had been his job, his identity, his reason for being in the world, but then he'd gotten wounded and ended up with a medical discharge, and his life had changed forever. He'd been adrift. Rudderless. Hopeless. He couldn't make plans for a future when he no longer knew who or what he was.

In the back of his mind, there had lurked this amorphous "one day." One day he would meet the right woman. One day he would settle down. One day he would have children. But the truth was, he hadn't known how to do those things. He'd married Shaina out of lust and loneliness, but he'd honestly had no idea how to be a husband. Yes, she'd cheated on him, but she hadn't been 100 percent to blame. He'd been too married to the army to be a proper husband.

But when Tara kissed him, he felt a quiet peace settle deep inside him. She made him believe that he could have anything he wanted. Be anything he chose to be. She made him hope again. Her optimism offered him a lifeline.

She splayed her palms and ran them up his back.

Oh yeah, sweetheart. Touch me. Touch me all over.

He was so hard he ached right down to the very root of his manhood. Her hands were so hot, her mouth so encouraging, and her sweet little moans shot him into orbit.

She broke their contact, pressed her mouth to his ear and whispered in a breath that drove him insane, "Take me to bed, Boone. Take me there now."

12

THE HEAT ROLLING off his body seeped into her. She pressed against Boone, desperate to have him inside her and terrified that he would refuse her invitation. She knew this was only for tonight. Just for now, but she was okay with that. Having him for a few hours was better than never having him at all.

She loved the way he made her feel—feminine, cherished, treasured. Who would have thought such a big, rugged man could be so tender?

He pressed his burning lips to her forehead. "Tara, I want you so badly I can't think straight, but my knee—"

"I'll be on top," she interrupted.

"I don't have any condoms on me."

"I do."

"You carry condoms with you?" He sounded both amused and alarmed.

"I might be impulsive, but I'm not stupid."

"I never said that."

"Give me just a sec." She stumbled around in the dark, trying to find her overnight bag and worried the delay would give him too much time to think. She didn't want him backing out on her. She whacked into the desk chair. "Ouch."

"Be careful, sweetheart."

Sweetheart! Boone had just called her *sweetheart!*
Don't read anything into it.

But how could she not? Boone was most definitely not the type to casually toss around terms of endearment. What did it mean?

Doesn't matter what it means. His life is in Montana, you're moving home to start over. You know well enough that long-distance relationships never work out. That's why you moved to Montana in the first place.

Except *that* relationship had not worked out either.

Forget all that. Find your bag, get the condom and get back to that hunky man.

She tripped over her bag, almost went down but managed to get her balance. Her toe throbbed. "Shoot."

"You okay?" His voice wrapped around her in the darkness.

"Fine, fine." *I will be perfect as soon as I've got you on your back in that bed.*

Except she was so nervous—she'd been fantasizing about sleeping with him for months—she fumbled the condom, dropped it and had to feel around on the floor. She was so not the queen of smooth moves.

"You thinking of backing out on me, sweetheart?" There was a low, throaty humor in his voice.

Her head shot up. "No!"

"That sounds definitive."

"It is. I am. Definitive. I wanna do this."

"Good to know your heart's in it."

Finally, her hand brushed against the foil packet and

she closed her fist over it. *Gotcha.* Now she had to find her way back to bed.

"This way," Boone guided, reading her mind. He had an uncanny knack for anticipating her needs. His skill unsettled her at the same time it pleased her.

Don't get used to it.

She found him by sense of smell. Every time she caught a whiff of his cologne, it touched something deep inside of her.

"Tara," he murmured and his hand found her in the darkness.

She was worried that he'd lost his desire, but that fear was laid to rest the minute he pulled her against his chest. His strong arms encircled her, made her feel safe and protected as if nothing could touch her as long as she was in his embrace.

He kissed her as his hand tugged at her T-shirt, working it up over her head. Every nerve in her body came alive. Tara shivered as his mouth moved slowly from her lips to her throat. Her top disappeared and his fingers went to the tie of her yoga pants.

"Let me help," she said, shucking off her pants and tossing them over her shoulders.

Boone laughed at her eagerness, a buoyant sound that warmed her heart.

Tara pushed her hands up his bare chest, her fingers getting caught in the tuft of springy masculine hair running across his pecs. She hissed in appreciation. "Sex-*y.*"

"Yes, you are," he murmured and cupped her breasts in his hands.

She giggled and wriggled against him, pulling a groan from his throat. She wished she could see him. They were breathing rapidly, inhaling and exhaling in the same hurried rhythm. The darkness sensitized every touch, taste, sound and smell. Who needed to see when every other sense was heightened so acutely?

His calloused palms skimmed over her breasts. His taste made her think of popcorn, salty and delicious. The sounds he made had her picturing a powerful male. And his scent—so masculine and musky—filled her nose and stirred the need in her.

He pulled her up tight against his chest, pressing her to his hard angles that promised so much. She tilted her head and planted a kiss on the underside of his chin.

Awareness sparked off them, brilliant as the lightning flashing in erotic intervals, giving just a quick glimpse of bare flesh. She gripped the hard muscles of his biceps, dug her fingernails into his skin.

Desire burned her veins, yanked her high on an upsurge of sexual need, flung her obliviously toward a sweet, dark destiny. Her womb clenched, eager for him.

His erection stabbed against her pelvis, the hard ridge of him raising excited goose bumps on her arms.

Tara moaned softly and ground her hips against his.

He pulled her head down to nibble her earlobe, and growled into her ear. A jolt of sexual longing seized her. He pushed his hips against her, his erection offering sensual promises of what was to come.

She wanted this.

Wanted him.

Not just wanted, but needed. She needed him.

His hand slipped between their bodies pressed so closely together, and he gently pushed his thick middle finger inside of her, stroking her ache.

She nipped his shoulder and then sank her teeth lightly into his flesh.

Groaning, he touched her in places that ignited a

thousand tiny fires up and down her skin and pushed his finger in deeper, stoking her fever.

She was so swept away she could barely open the condom, and when she moved to roll it on his throbbing erection, her hands were shaking so hard he had to take the condom from her and put it on himself.

Once he was sheathed, his mouth caught hers again in a possessive kiss that made her quiver from the inside out. They were lost in the headiness of the moment.

Her tingling fingers skated down the masculine angles and hard-ridged muscles of his torso.

He had a hand on her bottom and drew her up tight against his hardness, and she just became one with the dark mystery of the storm. Boone put his hands around her waist. "So tiny," he breathed as he leveled her up onto him.

She was hot and ready and slipped over him with amazing ease. Slowly she slid down, and when she'd taken him all the way, Boone let out a rough sigh. Her feminine muscles contracted around him.

"Hold off a bit on that," he said in a strangled voice totally lacking in control. "If you don't want this to be over in sixty seconds."

She tried to comply, but he felt so good, so big and thick and wonderful that she couldn't resist giving him another squeeze.

"You're playing with fire." His voice was tight, edgy.

"I'll be good," she agreed.

"You're incredible," he said. "I'm not sure you're aware of just how incredible you are."

"Not as incredible as you are," she replied saucily and squeezed him again to remind him she could make or break him.

He groaned. "Wench."

Slowly, she began to move over him, marveling at how well they fit. It was as if she'd been created for him and he for her. Like two pieces of a puzzle, snug together. Two joined pieces made whole.

He took her hand and brought it to his mouth, kissing each knuckle before taking her thumb between his lips and slowly sucking on it. It was wildly sensual and caused her thighs to tighten around his waist.

She rocked over him, taking every manly inch.

"You're driving me mad, woman."

"Ha! You've picked up on my evil plan."

"Two can play that game." He raised his head while at the same time tugging her down until his mouth captured one of her taut nipples.

The sensation that shot through her body was wickedly otherworldly. As he suckled her, he arched his hips upward.

Craving spurred her on. She rocked hard, undone by the tingling current running from her nipples to her womb as he continued to lick and tease her breast. Clearly, he was trying to drive her insane with passion. She could feel the storm coming, gathering in her primal core, rumbling up from deep within her.

His hot mouth destroyed any last shred of sanity she possessed. Tara wrapped her arms around his neck, holding on for dear life. He worked her over, showed no mercy. It was a beautiful, mind-blowing bliss.

She quickened the pace until they were both grunting and writhing, both barely hanging on.

He tugged her down to him and kissed her, hard and demanding. She tasted his desperate need, shocked by how much he wanted her. Stunned by how much she wanted him.

"Tara," he called her name. "Tara," he called again.

His body stiffened. She egged him on with hot little gasps and soft, hungry moans. Her contractions held him tight, pulling her down deeper onto him, claiming him as her own.

Tension reached a fever pitch.

She gripped him with her thighs. He cupped her buttocks in his hands, moved her up and down on him.

Then abruptly, it happened. They exploded together. Tara felt the lightning. Tasted the thunder. Flew into the eye of the storm. And in the bliss of that magnificent burst, Tara realized she'd done the unthinkable.

She'd fallen in love.

BOONE LAY IN THE darkness, the back of his head propped in the palms of his hands, listening to the storm—both internal and external—roll away. His knee was throbbing, but it was worth a little pain to feel what he'd just experienced.

Also worth the pain was the woman sleeping with her head on his chest.

She's not yours to keep.

Too bad, because he couldn't remember the last time a woman fascinated him the way Tara did. She delighted him. Made him laugh. And these days, that was no small task. She brought him out of the dark place where he'd been living and into the light. She was the most open, spontaneous person he'd ever met.

He thought he heard a noise in the parking lot. Banging noises. The alert, protector part of him had an urge to go check and see what was going on, but he didn't want to disturb Tara. Besides, hadn't she accused him of thinking it was his responsibility to police the world? It was probably nothing more than something knocked loose in the storm hitting the side of the motel. He imag-

ined Tara teasing him for always suspecting the worst
and quelled his impulse to investigate. The things he
would do to please her. He'd walk over hot coals barefoot if she asked him to, with a smile on his face, singing "Yankee Doodle Dandy."

Lightly, so as not to wake her, he turned his head and
softly kissed her forehead. How had he ended up here,
with his heart all tangled up in her?

Ah, hell. He'd done what he'd resisted for months.
He'd fallen for her. Wasn't that a kick in the teeth?

His mind whirled as he struggled to think of a way to
make this thing between them work, but each thought
ended up in the same place. He wasn't ready to be in
love. He was a mess, both physically and emotionally.
Healing, yes, but still in no position to start a romance.

*Too late. You're in bed with her after the most ter-
rific sex of your life.*

Panic took hold of him then and he had a powerful
urge to slip from the bed and run away into the night.
Two things stopped him. One, he couldn't run anywhere
with his damn leg. And two, he wasn't the kind of guy
who ran away from trouble.

A hopeful part of him that he'd thought had disappeared ages ago started trying to figure out how a long-
distance relationship might work. Or better yet, how he
could convince her to take that U-Haul right back to
Montana after this was over.

Mentally, he crushed the hope. Shut it down. He'd
learned the hard way how dangerous hope could be.

"Boone?" Tara whispered. "Are you awake?"

"Yes."

"The storm's passed."

Not the storm in my heart. Great. Now he was thinking like a sap.

Fingertips walked up the middle of his chest. "Mmm," Tara said. "Would you be interested in doing that again?"

Instantly, he was aroused. "Maybe that's not such a good idea."

"Why not?"

"Let's not make this any more complicated than it is."

"What's complicated about it?" she murmured. "I want you…" She reached down and touched his erection. "You want me. Pretty simple equation in my book."

Boone closed his eyes, pressed his lips together. "So just to be clear, this is simply about casual sex?"

"Absolutely," she said so quickly that any lingering hope he was entertaining vanished.

He should have known better. He was dumb for even thinking that what they'd done could mean more to her. She was footloose, a spontaneous, free spirit. It was one of the things he loved most about her. He could no more tie her down than he could cage the wind.

She moved to kiss him and he made the fatal mistake of letting her. He was helpless against those lips. She tasted so damned good.

She was pressing her hot little mouth into the center of his chest and slowly edging downward. All the blood drained from his head, shot straight to his groin. "Please," she begged between each kiss.

It killed him that he couldn't flip her over onto her back, sink his body into hers and stare into her eyes while he claimed her fully and completely. When her mouth made contact with the hardest part of him, he lost all ability to think.

A groan escaped his lips.

The next thing he knew, she was straddling him backward, her knees on either side of him. Her fanny in

the air, her head down between his thighs, her tongue—
oh, damn, that glorious tongue—licking him hotly.

He rose up and braced himself on his elbows to press
his lips to one saucy cheek. Her skin was so soft there,
and she smelled like sweet sin. While her mouth swirled
around and over his erection, Boone took matters into
his own hands.

She let out a gasp when his fingers dipped into her
damp flesh and he kissed the inside of her thigh. She
tasted as good as she smelled—all warm and feminine.
She gave as good as she got, though, making love to
him with her mouth, caressing him with her tongue,
coaxing him to the edge, then easing off.

Teasing. Taunting. Driving him crazy.

Fighting back, he flicked his tongue across the most
sensitive part of her and she made a high, needy sound
that cut him in two. He clutched both of her cheeks in
his palms. The sound deepened and she wriggled her
fanny closer to his mouth.

"You have no idea how long I've been dreaming
of doing this," he murmured and ran his lips over her
lovely folds, stroking her with his tongue, eagerly ex-
ploring everything she had to offer.

"Boone." She exhaled on a reedy sigh and proceeded
to do exactly the same thing to him until they were both
quivering and their breathing was raspy. "Yes. Oh, yes."

He loved the noises she was making, made a few of
his own. He loved the way she looked in the moonlight
that now spilled in through the open curtains. Gorgeous.
She was absolutely beautiful in every way.

They toyed with each other, using their mouths and
their fingers to coax the tension higher, hotter. He felt
the pressure climbing, pushing up through him, rushing to be released.

"That feels so good," she exclaimed. "Oh, Boone, what are you doing to me?"

"I'm on the same train, sweetheart."

"We're gonna crash hard."

"I know. I know!" Things were a crazy blur now—fast and hard and hot. They moaned and whimpered and writhed together. Boone surrendered everything to her. Right then. Right there. Handed his heart to her on a platter. He held nothing back.

When she swirled her tongue around him one final time, he knew he was going to lose everything. He felt the tragic, bittersweet melancholy of his loss at the same moment he reached the pinnacle of pure physical joy. He felt as if he'd just summited Everest in the clear, cold light of dawn, sun glimmering off the clouds, his spirit triumphant even as a part of him realized it was a long way back down that icy slope.

He wasn't the only one lost in the glory. Her body stiffened. "You… This… Great…" She gasped. "No other."

No other person had ever made him feel like this, either. Which was the bad part. She'd moved the bricks in front of his heart. Broken through his crusty exterior with her sweet sunshine. She'd laid him bare until he was utterly defenseless, and now she was just going to walk away, leaving him in a hundred little pieces. Leaving him raw and achy and bereft of her.

A hitching sigh explored from her lips at the same time he whispered her name. "Tara. Tara."

He was with her in every sense of the word—at least for this one splendid second. They burst together. It all felt so right, and then an ache like a fist punched his chest.

Because just as he found her, Boone knew he'd lost her.

By the end of the day, she'd be out of his life for good and he'd be alone again. The way he thought he'd wanted it. Now he knew he'd never wanted that at all.

THE CHUFFING Jake brakes of an eighteen-wheeler coming off the highway pulled Tara awake at dawn.

Opening her eyes, she sat up and looked over at Boone, the memory of what they'd shared the night before imprinted in her body, memory and soul. There was no escaping what they'd done. It could never be erased.

Not that she wanted to erase it. She would remember her time with him as the most special encounter of her life. Too bad things would never work out between them.

She cast a gaze over him.

He looked so handsome stretched out on the mattress, his shorter hair sexily tousled, fresh stubble sprouting at his jawline, the white sheet contrasting so sexily with his tanned skin. She licked her lips and longed for another kiss.

A flicker of hope flamed up inside her. *What if?* she started to wonder. But before her mind could start spinning impossible scenarios, she quickly doused the thought. They were worlds apart. He had his life in Montana. She was starting over again in Miami. Too bad they hadn't gotten together while she was in Bozeman. She might have considered staying. But it was too late for that. She had a job waiting. Her family was expecting her.

Most importantly—for all she knew Boone did not feel the same way about her. She might want him more than she'd ever wanted anything in her life, but she had her pride. She wouldn't throw herself at him. She couldn't make the man love her if he didn't and she wasn't about to say it first. Being the first to say "I love you" put you behind the eight ball. She simply didn't have that kind of courage. She was going to make leaving easy for him. She would never let him know that she'd fallen in love.

Coward.

Maybe so, but it was the only way she'd survive.

He opened one eye, caught her staring at him. "C'mere, you," he said and pulled her to him.

Her eyes closed as he planted his mouth against her throat. She should resist. Say no. Put a stop to it. They needed to get on the road. They needed—

But then he did this amazing thing with his tongue and every thought flew right out of her brain. He kissed her and kissed her and kissed her some more until she didn't know which way was up. He might not be in love with her, but he had a way of making her feel so protected, so cherished, so cared for. That was part of the problem. She couldn't rely on those feelings. They were just feelings. They would pass.

"Tara," he whispered, his voice incredibly husky.

"Uh-huh?" she managed in a dreamy whisper.

"Do you have any more of those condoms?"

"I WISH WE COULD stay here forever," Boone said a half hour later. "But we need to get on the road."

"Sure thing." Tara sprang from the bed as if relieved to have a reason to get away from him. She bustled around the room, packing up her belongings.

Slowly, Boone swung his legs to the floor, trying to ignore the heaviness settling in the bottom of his stomach.

Remember why you're here. You've got to get to Key West before Jackie makes the biggest mistake of her life.

It sounded good, but in reality, who was he to tell Jackie how to live her life? It wasn't as if he'd had the best success with his. Maybe Jackie had met the love of her life. Well, if that was the case, he wanted to be there to walk her down the aisle.

Fat chance with this bum knee.

He stared glumly at his leg.

"Do you need help putting this on?" Tara asked, holding out his leg brace.

"I've got it," he said gruffly.

"Okay." She held up both palms. "I'll go load our things in the car." Tara scooped up her overnight bag and his knapsack, shouldered them both and headed for the door. It was a humbling experience, letting her take care of things.

She paused at the door. "Boone?"

He met her eyes.

Then, as if reading his mind, she said, "Everyone needs help now and again. It's nothing to be ashamed of."

With a quick smile, she disappeared out the door.

Boone had just secured the straps of the brace around his leg when he heard a small, strangled cry of alarm. Instantly, he went on full alert. *Tara!*

Moving as fast as he could, he limped to the door and peered out.

What he saw dropped his heart into his shoes.

Tara was in the parking lot, both hands threaded through her hair as she stared in dismay at the U-Haul. The back door of the moving van trailer stood open. Inside, it was totally empty.

Guilt ground Boone into broken glass. While he'd

talked himself out of investigating the noises he'd heard, while they'd been in the motel room making love, someone had been robbing her blind.

And he'd allowed it to happen.

13

"EVERYTHING'S GONE," Tara murmured, trying to steel her chin so it didn't quiver. She didn't want to cry in front of Boone. She had a philosophy to uphold. Material things weren't important, right? They were just possessions, nothing that couldn't be replaced. Her clothes, her computer and television, her furniture and household items were gone, but no one had been hurt or maimed or killed.

Boone's hand settled on her shoulder, strong and reassuring. "I'm so sorry, sweetheart."

The term of endearment sent her stomach flip-flopping. Did he really mean it? Or was he just trying to be sympathetic? It wasn't the first time he'd called her that and he wasn't the kind of guy to throw the word around lightly, but she refused to read anything into it. He hadn't said a word about the future and she certainly wasn't going to bring it up and be the one to look pathetic if it turned out they weren't on the same page. Been there, done that, had the scorch marks to prove it. When it came to love, she assumed nothing.

Love.

There it was. Her stomach took another dip and whirl on the emotional trampoline. Good, bad or indifferent, she loved Boone Toliver. It had been coming for several weeks, but the road trip had cinched her feelings.

She loved his steadfastness. The way he had her back. She loved the way she felt around him, as if she had nothing to fear. She loved the way she lit up inside whenever he smiled at her. She craved his nearness, was addicted to his kisses and longed for his embrace.

Tara turned her head, met his gaze, saw the tenderness in the big alpha man's eyes. Saw the chinks in his armor and loved him anyway. Saw past the barriers he'd erected to the huge-hearted guy who was so afraid of love, but so lonely in his isolation. Loved him because of his vulnerabilities.

She also knew that love wasn't enough. She could love him all she wanted, but she could not cure him. He had to do that on his own. The only thing she could do was give him the opportunity to heal himself and that started with making sure he got to his sister's wedding in time. She could not hold him back. He had his own life, his own path, his own agenda. The sound of footsteps slapping against the damp pavement drew Tara's gaze from Boone as she shifted her attention to Raj, the desk clerk who'd checked them in the night before.

"When I arrived at work this morning I saw what had happened to your valuables and I immediately called law enforcement. They are delayed because of problems created by last night's storm," Raj said, an apologetic expression on his face. "But they are on the way."

"Thank you." Tara gave him a faint smile.

"We assume no responsibility for theft," he added quickly.

"I'm not blaming anyone." Tara struggled to keep the smile on her face. "These things happen."

"We want to see the footage of your surveillance camera." Boone nodded at the setup mounted on the building overlooking the parking lot.

Raj shifted, dropped his gaze. "I'm not authorized—"

"Show it to us," Boone commanded in such a take-charge voice Tara's heart strummed. She loved it when he got all protective.

"Um…" A chagrined expression crossed the desk clerk's face. "The cameras don't work. Vandals." He shrugged.

"Listen here." Boone took a step toward the man, who cringed.

"It's all right." Tara rested a hand on Boone's arm. "Truly. What's important now is for you to find another way to Key West. Clearly, I'm going to be tied up here for a long while."

Boone glanced at his watch and then met her gaze. "There's no way I can make it."

"You are in luck! There's a bus stop across the street," Raj said.

"What are the chances there will be one headed to Key West in time?"

"There is an express bus that comes through here at 7:30 a.m. headed for Miami. I know this because I have worked here for three years and every morning the bus drives by with the sign 'Miami' lit up," Raj said eagerly, as if he couldn't wait to get Boone on any bus to anywhere as long as it wasn't here.

"It's seven-twenty," Tara said "It's fated. You can catch a cab to Key West from Miami."

"I thought you said when Mercury was in retrograde that it affected travel plans."

"Even more evidence this is fated. Go," she insisted.

"It will take too long. I'll never make it. I'll try to call Jackie." He pulled his cell phone from his pocket. "Maybe she's over being mad at me and will answer this time."

"She hasn't answered once this entire trip. I'll be fine. The cops will show up, I'll file a report and be back on the road in a few hours. It's your only chance. Go."

At that moment, a big silver bus came off the highway exit ramp.

"Fate," she said. "You better hurry."

"But I can't leave you alone, not when you're in trouble," he protested.

"Seriously, go. I'll be fine."

"She'll be fine," Raj echoed.

Boone glowered at Raj who cowered, and then he glanced over at the bus coming to a gradual stop.

"Go," Tara said firmly, even though she wanted him to stay. She felt lost and lonely, but fate had spoken. Boone was supposed to be in Key West. Honestly, it was better this way. No long goodbye. Then she added, just to make sure he went, "Hey, you're getting on my last nerve. I don't need you. Hit the road, Jack."

BOONE BOARDED the bus with a guilty conscience. He hated going off and leaving Tara alone. She hadn't fooled him with her bluster. He knew she was just trying to make him catch the bus. If Jackie weren't getting married today, nothing else on earth would have made him leave Tara, but, well, his baby sister was getting married, and if he couldn't talk her out of it, he at least wanted to be there for her. As self-absorbed as Jackie's father was, Boone might be the only relative she had at the nuptials.

His time with Tara had taught him a few things. Lessons he was surprised to learn. Like maybe he didn't have all the answers. When had he become such a know-it-all? What surprised him most was that Tara didn't judge him for his tendency to assume his way was the right way, she just showed him how he was putting up barriers between himself and his sister.

Her wisdom shook him. In spite of her frivolous appearance and Pollyanna attitude, she was far wiser than he. She'd shown him that he didn't have to shoulder every burden and that if he let others help him, life could be so much easier. What he'd mistaken as a weakness in her—depending on friends and family—was, in fact, strength. He was the weak one, isolating himself from those who cared about him.

He wished now that he'd told her this, paid her the compliments she so richly deserved, but it was too late.

You could always write to her. Call her. Text her.

Yeah, but he knew he wouldn't. Why keep up the torture? It was better to let her go than cling to the ridiculous hope that he was anything more to her than a temporary adventure.

Boone stared out the window as the bus pulled away and scanned the motel parking lot, eager for one last glimpse of Tara, but she was nowhere in sight. He let out a disappointed sigh, leaned back against the seat and closed his eyes.

"Muffin?"

He opened one eye and peered at the elderly woman sitting beside him. She smiled and held up a cellophane package with two banana-nut muffins. "I won't eat them both, and I do so hate to waste food. You look so exhausted I thought you could use a pick-me-up."

It wasn't health-food fare. Boone was about to say "No, thank you," but then he thought of what Tara had said. *People love to help. It makes them feel good about themselves. Why do you cheat people out of the opportunity to feel good about themselves?*

"Yes, ma'am." He nodded. "That's very kind of you."

She beamed and passed him a muffin. "Where you headed?"

"Key West."

Her eyes twinkled. "To see a girlfriend?"

"No, ma'am. My sister's getting married."

"That's so nice. Weddings are so lovely." She sighed dreamily. "You don't have a girlfriend?"

He thought of Tara, shrugged.

"Ah, you've just broken up. I'm sorry." She patted his arm.

"It's for the best," he was surprised to hear himself say. He and Tara hadn't broken up. They'd never been together.

What do you call last night?

Red-hot sex. That's all it had been.

Yeah, right. If you keep lying long enough, you'll start believing your own fairy tales.

"Why did you break up? Did she cheat on you?"

"No. Tara is the most loyal person I've ever met."

"The sex was no good?" she asked impishly. "What? Don't look shocked. I know how important sex is to a man. My Henry, God rest his soul, was dynamite in the sack."

Boone's cheeks heated, couldn't believe what he was admitting to this stranger. "The sex *was* phenomenal."

"Was she a spendthrift? Blew all your money?"

He shook his head. "In fact, she's pretty frugal, just like I am."

"Hmm." A speculative expression crossed the woman's face.

"'Hmm' what?"

"Sounds to me like you're still in love with her. You couldn't work out your differences? True love is more precious than gold."

"It's a long-distance relationship."

"So move."

"It's not that simple."

The woman snorted.

"She believes planetary alignment affects travel plans."

"And you're pragmatic."

He nodded. "She's so cheerful, it's irritating."

"And you're a bit of a grouch."

"She's outgoing."

"And you're an introvert."

"Yeah. Total opposites."

The woman's smile turned coy. "Opposites attract for a reason. People mistakenly think relationships should be smooth sailing, but our true soul mates challenge us to be our best selves. When we're challenged there's always rough seas, but without challenge, we don't learn and grow."

"I suppose," he said and purposefully focused on the muffin. He'd just finished it off—and damn but the muffin was tasty and he was hungry—when they heard a loud bang and the bus jolted to a sudden, shuddering halt, gears screaming and grinding.

Acting on pure instinct, Boone threw himself over the elderly woman to protect her from whatever was happening in the front of the bus as people gasped and hollered and jumped from their seats. One terrifying scenario after another surged through his head. Bomb. Gunman. Terrorists.

"My goodness!" the woman exclaimed. "What's going on?"

"Are you all right?" he asked her.

"I'm fine, but my muffin got smashed." She held up the flattened snack.

"Stay put," he told the muffin woman and dragged himself around her and out into the aisle. Boone scanned the bus, alert for enemies. He wished he had a gun.

Alarmed passengers were hugging each other, grabbing for their belongings, most of them talking at once. Some people had their cell phones out and were videotaping the chaos.

"What's happening?"

"Did we crash?"

"Is anyone hurt?"

The bus driver got to his feet. "Settle down, folks, just a little mechanical glitch, nothing to get alarmed about. Please stay seated. I'll be right back."

No one sat back down.

The driver got off the bus. A few male passengers got off behind him. Boone would have gotten off, too, if he hadn't been so far in the back and it was so difficult getting down the crowded aisle with his bum leg.

A few minutes later the driver returned. "We've lost the drive shaft," he said.

A chorus of groans and boos went up from the passengers.

"Calm down. I've radioed in and they'll have another bus here within the hour. Please just sit back down."

"Maybe there's something to your girlfriend's planetary alignment theory," the muffin lady said.

Mercury in retrograde. Fate. Whatever you wanted to call it, Boone didn't care. This was his opportunity to go back and see this through with Tara. He had no hope of getting to Key West before four o'clock anyway.

Urgency pushed at him and Boone retrieved his knapsack from the overhead bin and started toward the door.

"Sir, sir, where are you going?" the driver asked.

"Nowhere," he said. "I'm staying right here. Please open the door."

"Sir—"

"The door," Boone commanded.

Reluctantly, the driver opened the door.

Boone stepped off the bus, the oppressive feeling that had been pressing down on him ever since he climbed on the bus dissipating the minute his feet hit the ground. He was going back to Tara.

That was when he realized the error of his ways. The motel was a good five miles away and he had a bad leg. By the time he walked back, she might very well be gone.

TARA SAT ON the curb at the motel trying not to feel sorry for herself. She hummed a tune and forced herself to smile. How long was it going to take the cops to show up?

Boone was gone, on the highway headed for his destiny. She could be happy about that. At least he wasn't stuck here with her. That was a good thing. He'd get to Key West and find his sister. They would talk things out. Repair their relationship. She'd done a good thing.

Why, then, did she feel so crappy?

Because she missed Boone something terrible.

Sadness swept over her. It was all she could do not

to cry. She blinked and pressed her palm to the back of her mouth. Her nose grew stuffy with unshed tears. *Stop it, stop it, stop it.*

A police car turned into the motel parking lot.

At last!

Tara got to her feet, dusting her fanny.

The cruiser stopped. The back door opened and out stepped Boone.

Joy flooded over her. It was all she could do to keep from running across the pavement and flinging herself into his arms. Restraining herself, she sauntered casually over.

"Hi," she said breathlessly.

"Hi." He grinned.

"You came back."

"The bus broke down."

"Oh, no."

"Well, Mercury is in retrograde," he pointed out.

"You don't believe in that."

"It killed me thinking about you here all by yourself. Facing this alone." He waved at the empty U-Haul. "I started walking back from the bus."

"How far away were you?"

"Five miles.

"Boone! Your leg is healing. You can't walk five miles!"

"Plus, apparently it's illegal to walk along the highway in Florida."

"It's for your safety."

"Luckily, the officers who stopped to tell me that I was breaking the law were on their way over here and they took pity on a war vet."

"Imagine that."

"Fate," Boone said.

"You don't believe in that, either."

"Maybe not," he said. "But I believe in you. I'm gonna stay with you and see things through."

"You're going to miss Jackie's wedding."

He blew out his breath. "Can't be helped."

"Fate has other plans."

"If you say so."

He linked his arm through hers and guided her over to the officers climbing from the cruiser. Grinning, Tara leaned into him, and even though she'd just lost everything she owned, she couldn't help feeling that this was one of the best days of her life.

WITH THE POLICE report filled out, they were on the road again. Tara was singing an off-key version of "On the Road Again," and Boone couldn't help feeling it was the best rendition he'd ever heard. Hell, he couldn't stop darting glances over at her. Mainly, he couldn't help being grateful that he had eked out a little more time with her. But grateful as he was, he almost had to admit that this made things that much harder.

It was almost ten o'clock by the time they left the small Florida town that was just over the Georgia border, where they'd spent the night and Tara was driving five miles over the speed limit. "I think we can make it. Fate is on our side, after all. I'll get you to your sister's wedding on time if we don't make any stops," she promised.

"It's out of your way," he said. "You're only going as far as Miami. I'd always planned on taking a taxi from Miami to Key West."

"Seriously, Boone, have you not met me? I go out of my way for my friends." She gave a little shrug. "For better or worse, it's just who I am. Friendships are important to me."

"And I'm your friend?"

"Aren't you?" She met his gaze.

Well, no. What he felt for her was far more than friendly. Which was the problem. No matter how hard he'd tried to resist her, he wasn't about to get out of this unscathed. "Yeah," he said, hearing the sarcasm in his voice. "We're friends."

"Friends with benefits," she added.

"What does that even mean?"

"You know. We're friends who make love."

"Do you have a lot of those? Friends with benefits?"

"No," she said. "Only you."

"I'm not sure that's such a good idea," he said.

She gulped visibly. "What? Friends with benefits, or friends?"

"Either one."

"Oh," she said and made a sad frowny face. He felt as if he'd ruined her party, but he had to do this. Had to make it clear that after today it would be far too painful to stay friends with her. A clean break was the best way.

Yeah, so why didn't you stay on the bus?

Because she'd needed him and, as dumb as the impulse was, he could never resist anyone in need.

"We're peas in a pod, you know."

He snorted. "We're nothing alike."

"On the surface, maybe not. You're a card-carrying Republican. I don't give two hoots about politics. You're closed off. I'm an open book. You're quiet and self-contained. I'm energetic and need to be around people."

He thought of what the muffin lady had said on the bus. *Opposites attract.*

"Neither one of us can turn away from someone in

need. Both of us value saving over spending. We're both great shots. We have a strong commitment to family—"

"That's where you're wrong."

"Of course you do. You're making this journey because you care so much about your sister. You feel disengaged from her and that bothers you a lot. If you didn't have a strong commitment to family, it wouldn't concern you at all. And who sat at his father's bedside every single day while he lay dying? Yes, Mrs. Levison told me about that."

Boone shifted uncomfortably.

"And," she pointed out, "compliments make us both uneasy. Mainly because neither one of us do the things we do for praise, but because it makes us feel good. That's why I'm taking you to Key West. But most of all, we're great in bed together."

He couldn't argue with that. "That's the problem, Tara. Because of how damn good we make each other feel, I can't simply be your friend or friends with benefits. I'd need more from you."

"Really?" she said breathlessly.

"Yeah and the distance between us doesn't allow for that."

"My mom needs me."

"I know. Family commitment comes first."

"Yes," she said.

He wanted to say that maybe after things were settled with her mother they could pick up where they left off, but he knew that wasn't true. Too much time would have passed. Too much would have changed. Tara would be back with her family. Her old friends. Soon enough he would be nothing but a pleasant memory. Part of him wanted to throw caution to the wind and say, "Hell, I'll move to Miami to be with you," but that sounded too much like begging. She hadn't given him any indication she wanted him here. Had, in fact, made several comments about keeping things light. And that friends-with-benefits mess. Totally unacceptable.

"Maybe you could come visit me," she said. "When you can fly again."

"Maybe," he echoed, knowing he was lying.

"You will be coming back to Florida after all, once you make a deeper connection with your sister."

"That's probably not going to happen. Especially when I try to talk her out of getting married."

"You're probably right. Best just to tuck this relationship in the memory banks and let it go," Tara said and fell silent.

And for the next six hours, neither one of them said another word.

_14_

BY THE TIME THEY reached Key West the car was thick with tension. Boone's muscles were coiled tight as he imagined what he would say to Jackie. He gave Tara directions to the wedding venue, fisted his hands against his thighs, and kept his eyes on the car's digital clock. Tara had gotten him here in record time, with fifteen minutes to spare.

She stopped the Honda beside the wharf where the *Sea Anemone* was docked. "Go find her."

"You're not coming?"

"I'll find a place to park and wait right here until you're done."

He wanted her with him, but felt he had no right to ask.

She rested her hand on his shoulder. "It's a family matter, Boone. Go."

He nodded, but couldn't help wishing that she were part of the family so that she could be involved. His leg had gone to sleep, but he had to get to Jackie. He got out of the car and hobbled toward the *Sea Anemone*. The parking area was packed.

When he reached the ramp leading to the ship, he cast one last glance over his shoulder and saw Tara pulling the U-Haul around. She stuck her hand out the window and waved. He could almost hear her. *Go.*

Funny. Now that he was here, on the verge of achieving his goal, he was no longer sure he wanted it. Who was he to tell Jackie how to live her life?

Taking a deep breath, he boarded the ship, only now becoming aware of how ragtag he must look in a T-shirt and cargo shorts, his knee brace, with his hair mussed and his jawline whisker-laden.

Greeters stood at the door handing out programs as guests trickled aboard the ship, many of them wearing Coast Guard dress uniforms.

"Can you tell me where to find the bride?" Boone asked a slender young woman dressed in buttercup-yellow.

"She's getting ready in the galley," the woman explained. "But the ceremony is about to start."

Boone limped toward the galley as fast as he could, his heart thumping, his mind racing as he tried out the speeches he'd rehearsed in his head on the drive down. Outside the galley he paused, and then knocked forcefully on the door.

"Who is it?" came a feminine voice.

"Is the bride in there?" Boone asked.

The door opened and a dark-haired woman peered out at him. "Yes."

"Can I speak to her?"

The woman glanced at her watch. "There's really no time."

"It's important."

"Boone?" Jackie's voice called to him from inside the room.

He stepped past the woman, crossed the threshold and saw his sister standing there in a white dress. She looked so beautiful and so damned happy.

"You came!" she exclaimed, and the fight they'd had dissolved just like that.

"You look…" He shook his head. "Radiant."

"I feel radiant."

He lumbered across the room, swept her into his arms for a hug.

"Your leg," she exclaimed when he let her go. "What happened?"

"I had to have a third surgery." He shrugged.

"Why didn't you tell me?"

"I didn't want to worry you."

She linked her arm through his, rested her head on his shoulder. "I'm so happy you're here. You're going to love Scott."

"Jackie…" He paused and cast a glance at the other woman who was hovering at the door. "Can I speak to you alone?"

"Megan," Jackie said to her friend, "can you give us a couple of minutes?"

"It's five minutes to four," Megan said.

"We'll be quick." Jackie smiled and Megan left the room.

Boone took his sister by the shoulders and looked into her eyes. "Are you sure you're doing the right thing? You've only known this guy a few weeks."

"People spend their lives searching for true love," Jackie said. "But the truth is that we're all so blind. We don't find someone who is magically right for us. We're in each other's hearts all along and we recognize each other when we meet."

"That's very metaphysical, Jacks, and not very scientific."

"There are a lot of things in this world that science can't explain. Love is one of those things."

Was this his sister the marine biologist speaking? "Now you sound like my friend Tara," he mumbled.

Friend. He'd called Tara his friend.

"You've got a girlfriend?" Jackie grinned.

"Don't start matchmaking." He raised his palms. "This is your day, and I just want to make sure you know what you're doing."

Jackie notched her chin up. "I do."

"Are you sure?"

"Boone," Jackie said, "when you find someone you love, truly love and trust, it's the most beautiful gift in the entire world. I know you think that you had that with Shaina, but you didn't. You might have loved her, but you couldn't trust her. Unless you have trust, love won't survive. I trust Scott with my life."

He trusted Tara like that.

"You hang on to the past too tightly, Boone. Just let go. Let things unfold naturally."

He certainly had no control over Tara. She went through life like a butterfly on the breeze, beautiful, sailing, happy.

He knew now why he'd initially resisted and resented her cheerful happiness. It was because he so desperately longed to be like her but feared that he could never be. And he was terrified that by being with her, he'd capture his sweet, beautiful butterfly in a jar and she'd die beating her wings against the glass.

"When you're with the right person, your heart knows it." Jackie placed her palm flat over his chest.

His gaze locked with his sister's.

"Mom messed us up when she abandoned us," Jackie said. "But we can't allow her mistakes to define who we are. I'm taking a chance on marriage because it's worth the gamble. Don't let your fear keep you from finding love, Boone."

He touched her cheek. "How did you get so wise, little sister?"

She smiled and said one word. "Love."

TARA SAT IN the nearby parking lot and decided she wasn't going to keep her word. She wasn't going to wait around for Boone to come back. He was with family now. He'd be okay. It was time for her to go home. She took a deep breath, started the engine and was just about to pull out when she spied Boone limping toward her.

The sight of him squeezed her heart, just as it always did.

He came over to the driver's-side window. "Come on."

"Are you serious? I'm dressed like a beach bum."

"So am I. No one cares. But if you'd feel more comfortable, Jackie says she has a dress you can change into. They're holding the wedding for us. Come on."

She shook her head. The last thing she wanted was to see some bride and groom in love when her own heart was breaking. "No, Boone. This is your family event."

"Please," he said. "I want you there."

"There's no point. You said yourself that we weren't going to be friends."

"I was wrong about that. Come inside with me, we'll talk about it later."

"I don't think so."

"Please, sweetheart." He held out his hand.

What could she say to that? Tara killed the engine and got out. That's when she realized she was shaking.

Boone held out his hand and she took it, then slowly they walked onboard the ship together.

Three hours later they sat at a table at the reception at a nearby pavilion overlooking the ocean. They'd just finished a lovely meal. The toasts had been given. Glasses had been raised. The music and dancing had begun. Everyone who'd been sitting at their table was up on the dance floor. Tara was bobbing in her seat in time to a dreamy love ballad. She was wearing a blue sleeveless dress that Jackie had loaned her. It fit perfectly.

"Would you like to dance?" Boone asked.

"You can't dance." She pointed at his leg.

"We can stand on the dance floor and sway."

"Your leg has been put through enough for one day."

He got up, held out his hand. "May I have this dance?"

What was the point? Why was she here? The romantic wedding had been tough enough to get through, plucking at her tattered heartstrings. She was happy for Jackie and Scott, but dammit, she wanted her own happily-ever-after.

Wanted it with the man who was extending his hand.

Swallowing past the lump in her throat, she took his hand and let him lead her onto the dance floor just as the song ended.

"This next song goes out to Boone and Tara," the band's lead singer said into the microphone.

Tara looked at Boone. "You requested a song?"

His eyes darkened and he nodded.

The band launched into "Can't Help Falling in Love."

Her chest knotted up, tears burned her eyes. "Boone," she whispered.

"Tara," he answered, his eyes latching on to hers, electrifying her.

Was he telling her that he was falling in love with her? Could it be true that he felt the same thing she was feeling? He cradled her cheek in his palm. She tried to hang on to some shred of control just in case he was not saying that, but why would he have requested that song from the band?

"I was wrong," he said.

"About what?" She tried to keep her smile light, just in case this was all about to crumble around her.

"I think we should be friends."

"Oh?"

"Not just friends."

She arched her eyebrows. "Friends with benefits."

"Yes."

Her heart took a dip into her stomach. "I see."

"I want to be friends. I want the benefits." He winked. "But I want much more than that."

"When did this happen?"

"It's been happening for months, but I've been fighting it, denying it."

"Why is that?"

"'Cause I'm one stubborn man, but it wasn't until this trip and seeing my sister again that I realized the truth."

"And what is that?"

"There's nothing for me in Montana." He paused, moistened his lips, tightened his grip on her. "Everything I care about is here in Florida. My sister." He dipped his head and whispered in her ear, "My best friend."

Something happened inside her. It felt as if her chest

were caving in at the same time her heart was swelling so big she could not breathe. She could scarcely believe he was telling her these things.

He kissed her, slowly, gently, completely, then pulled back to gaze into her face again. "I love you, Tara Duvall. I love everything about you—the crazy color you paint your toenails, that sexy little wiggle of yours, the way you know how to use a pistol, how you hitch a ride from farmers on tractors and the way your smile lights up the morning. I love how thunderstorms make you run to me. But most of all, I love the way you invite people into your life with wide-open arms."

"Like this?" she said, and she held her arms wide and then wrapped him up close against her.

"Exactly like that," he said. "You are exactly what I've been waiting for my whole life, my perfect counterpoint, the other half of me."

"I love you, too, Boone Toliver. But you better watch out," she teased. "The next thing you know, you'll be telling me that you believe in fate."

"Sweetheart, you can make me believe that anything's possible." And with that he kissed her and sealed their fates together forever.

* * * * *

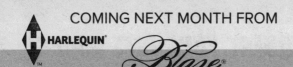

COMING NEXT MONTH FROM

HARLEQUIN *Blaze*

Available February 19, 2013

#739 A SEAL'S SURRENDER • *Uniformly Hot!*
by Tawny Weber
Cade Sullivan always knew he was meant to be a SEAL. Heck, he'd been pulling cute little Eden Gillespie out of scrapes from the time they were kids. But now Cade is home and Eden has turned into a *very* sexy woman. So who's going to save her this time—from him?

#740 MAKING HIM SWEAT
by Meg Maguire
When matchmaker Jenna Wilinski learns she's inherited a shady Boston boxing gym, she's not sure what to do. Suddenly, she's surrounded by men—hot and sweaty ones! But once she meets Mercer Rowley, she's tempted to work up a sweat herself....

#741 SIZZLE
by Kathy Garbera
Remy Stephens can whip up a feast of sensual delights, but so can Staci Rowland. These two reality show contestants are battling it out for the title of Premier Chef. But are they cooking up a storm in the kitchen—or in the bedroom?

#742 SMOOTH SAILING • *Stop the Wedding!*
by Lori Wilde
To convince his ex to give him another chance, reformed billionaire bad boy Jeb Whitcomb sets sail for Key West, only to fall for his accidental stowaway Haley French—the one woman he's never impressed, until now....

YOU CAN FIND MORE INFORMATION ON UPCOMING HARLEQUIN® TITLES, FREE EXCERPTS AND MORE AT WWW.HARLEQUIN.COM.

HBCNM0213

REQUEST YOUR FREE BOOKS!
2 FREE NOVELS PLUS 2 FREE GIFTS!

HARLEQUIN

Blaze

red-hot reads!

YES! Please send me 2 FREE Harlequin® Blaze™ novels and my 2 FREE gifts (gifts are worth about \$10). After receiving them, if I don't wish to receive any more books, I can return the shipping statement marked "cancel." If I don't cancel, I will receive 6 brand-new novels every month and be billed just \$4.49 per book in the U.S. or \$4.96 per book in Canada. That's a savings of at least 14% off the cover price. It's quite a bargain. Shipping and handling is just 50¢ per book in the U.S. and 75¢ per book in Canada.* I understand that accepting the 2 free books and gifts places me under no obligation to buy anything. I can always return a shipment and cancel at any time. Even if I never buy another book, the two free books and gifts are mine to keep forever.

151/351 HDN FVPV

Name	(PLEASE PRINT)	

Address		Apt. #

City	State/Prov.	Zip/Postal Code

Signature (if under 18, a parent or guardian must sign)

Mail to the **Harlequin® Reader Service:**
IN U.S.A.: P.O. Box 1867, Buffalo, NY 14240-1867
IN CANADA: P.O. Box 609, Fort Erie, Ontario L2A 5X3

Want to try two free books from another line?
Call 1-800-873-8635 or visit www.ReaderService.com.

* Terms and prices subject to change without notice. Prices do not include applicable taxes. Sales tax applicable in N.Y. Canadian residents will be charged applicable taxes. Offer not valid in Quebec. This offer is limited to one order per household. Not valid for current subscribers to Harlequin Blaze books. All orders subject to credit approval. Credit or debit balances in a customer's account(s) may be offset by any other outstanding balance owed by or to the customer. Please allow 4 to 6 weeks for delivery. Offer available while quantities last.

Your Privacy—The Harlequin® Reader Service is committed to protecting your privacy. Our Privacy Policy is available online at www.ReaderService.com or upon request from the Harlequin Reader Service.

We make a portion of our mailing list available to reputable third parties that offer products we believe may interest you. If you prefer that we not exchange your name with third parties, or if you wish to clarify or modify your communication preferences, please visit us at www.ReaderService.com/consumerschoice or write to us at Harlequin Reader Service Preference Service, P.O. Box 9062, Buffalo, NY 14269. Include your complete name and address.

HBI3

Jenna swallowed, her gaze dropping to Mercer's chest before she caught herself and hoisted it back up to his face. Shutting the cabinet, she mustered the nerve to ask, "How would you feel if I moved in before you moved out?"

"So, we'd be roommates until I find my next place?" When she nodded, he shrugged. "I guess I can put up with anybody for two weeks."

She looked down to hide her grin. She could sense him smiling back, could feel his closeness as tangibly as sunshine warming her skin. Dangerous.

"And hell," he said, leaning an arm along the door frame and bringing his face a little closer to hers, something hot and unwelcome spiking Jenna's pulse. Mercer smirked. "Maybe us shacking up together is just the chance I need to grow on you—change your mind about ruining all our lives."

Praying he couldn't see how his nearness had flushed her

cheeks, she ignored his challenge. "It'll save me a chunk of change on a hotel."

"You're the boss."

The boss. An intriguing notion. Boss to a small, inherited army of brutes for now. To a well-groomed team of assistants in a few weeks' time, all things going as planned.

In the sunlight, his hazel eyes were the warm, brownish-green of a ripe pear. His gaze was direct, intense as a flood-light. It seemed as though he was reading her thoughts. For a long moment, they just stared at one another. Too long a moment.

She swallowed, her gaze flitting from his bare arm to the shape of his chest, the stubble peppering his jaw and the curve of his lower lip. He mirrored the scrutiny, an expression of curiosity in his gaze.

"I've got an extra set of keys down in the office, if you want them today." His voice sounded so *close.*

"That'd be good." She inwardly sighed, feeling too many things. Overwhelmed, elated, terrified. *Attracted.* "Thank you," she said. "I know it's probably not easy being this courteous to me…."

"What choice have I got?"

"Because I'm your boss?"

"Nah. Because I loved your dad. And he loved you. So I have to at least pretend to respect your wishes." He grinned. "Although they really suck…."

Pick up MAKING HIM SWEAT by Meg Maguire, available February 19.